"What if they ask me about Laura and Hal?" I said to my uncle.

"You know what to say."

I followed him out to the hall. "I'm not exactly your normal all-American kid, am I? Sometimes I get the feeling it shows. Like pimples."

"Pete, calm down. Just go see your girl friend and put all that other stuff out of your mind."

"Stuff? You mean Laura and Hal? My parents? Is that what you'd do? Just wipe them out of the old mind? Blank them out as if they didn't exist? That's just great. That's really great!" I was suddenly shouting.

Other Avon Flare Books by
Norma Fox Mazer

MRS. FISH, APE, AND ME, THE DUMP QUEEN
TAKING TERRI MUELLER

DOWNTOWN

Norma Fox Mazer

AN AVON FLARE BOOK

AVON BOOKS
A division of
The Hearst Corporation
1790 Broadway
New York, New York 10019

Copyright © 1984 by Norma Fox Mazer
Published by arrangement with the author
Library of Congress Catalog Card Number: 84-91105
ISBN: 0-380-88534-4

First Avon Printing, September, 1984

AVON TRADEMARK REG. U. S. PAT. OFF. AND IN
OTHER COUNTRIES, MARCA REGISTRADA, HECHO EN
U. S. A.

Printed in the U. S. A.

WFH 10 9 8 7 6 5 4 3 2 1

For Karen and Jeff—love and hope.

"Kids with obsessed parents always pay a terrible price . . ."

Sidney Lumet, 1983

One

For a long time I've had these bad times that I call the White Terror. It usually happens to me in the morning after a long night of dreams. Murderous dreams; dreams of bodies lying headless and cold that I stumble over on some ordinary errand, on my way to school, or going into the bathroom, or down to the kitchen. In the dream I'm sometimes me as I am now, sometimes younger, but always moving along on some ordinary errand. And then I stumble over something hard yet mushy and I look down and there's a body, a headless rotting corpse. A paralyzing terror grips me. I can't move, can't run, can't go past the body or away from it. And as I stand there, my heart threatening to rip out of my chest, I feel myself dissolving, shrinking away into emptiness. And I scream, No! That's the point at which I wake up.

I'm always in a sweat, my heart whacking away, and as I thrash aside my covers, the emptiness is still there. And I wonder who I am, who is this person, this boy, this body? Am I real? Sometimes when it happens, I think I'm dying, but by now I know to just lie in bed until it subsides.

I was dead serious when I named it the White Terror, but I had to laugh when I found that same phrase, the White Terror, in a book I was reading about the Russian Revolution. After that, I tried calling *my* White Terror the American White Terror, but that sounded like a racist superhero. The American White Terror strikes again! Indeed, it does. And again and again, and never when I'm expecting it or telling myself to prepare for it. In between the times it happens, I try, only half successfully, to forget about it.

For a while I did magic things to keep it away, like always taking the same number of steps from our house to the corner. Or walking around the dining room table seven times when I came home from school. Or touching each corner of my bed as soon as I came into the room. Nothing helped. All I had to do—no, all I *could* do—was wait for it to come, wait for it to go. Well, why not? Half my life had been spent waiting. Waiting for word from my parents, waiting for their letters or the rare phone call. Waiting for this terror, this *thing,* to pass—was that so different?

I noticed that almost every time it happened, there was one small cool part of my brain that remained uninvolved. I dubbed it my Man Brain and began to think of it as the better part of me. I'd be sitting up in bed, gasping like a fish on land, with wave after wave of this emptiness and fear rolling over me, and my heart actually thumping so loud I could hear it, and all the time there was also that rational voice in my head, my Man Brain, telling me, *Your heart's beating . . . you're alive . . . you do exist . . . you are alive . . .*

The whole thing never actually lasts very long, maybe four or five minutes at the most. When it's over, that doesn't seem like much, but while it's happening, those four or five minutes are as long as eternity. Sometimes it ends abruptly, like a snap of the finger. Now you see it, now you don't. More often it goes like a fog slowly seeping away.

One morning I especially remember. I was sprawled in bed, in a stinking sweat, limp, shaking, the covers twisted around my legs, when, from across the hall, I heard my uncle clear his throat. *Eh, eh, ehhh.* I could *see* that sound, see it traveling through the wall of his bedroom into my room, see it bouncing off the bookcase, touching the desk, then slowly . . . slowly . . . sinking to the floor. It was agony, real agony, to watch that sound moving and wait for it to reach me.

Then it did. *Eh, eh, ehhh.* Just that, and the terror was gone. I was released. I lay there for a moment, letting it all go, then I was up and out of bed, whooping with relief. Instead of fifty push-ups, I did seventy-five, and I yelled across the hall to my uncle, "Gene, I want fried eggs this morning. French toast! Sausage! I'm a starving man!"

Released from the White Terror, I was—myself again. Someone real, who lived with his uncle, who had a name. No, two names: Pete Greenwood. Pax Martin Gandhi Connors.

But what did any of that matter? I was here and glad of the day, and for now, at least, the White Terror was gone.

Two

My uncle Gene's an optometrist by profession, an actor and gourmet cook by choice. One year the Winston Theatre Guild threw a fancy hundred-dollar-a-plate benefit dinner to raise money. Gene was the master chef with dozens of minor chefs scurrying around obsequiously, cutting and chopping and adding stuff to sauces, all under his direction. "Best role I've ever had," he said, afterward. "I felt like the White Queen. Off with their heads! Even if it was only parsley, the power kind of got to me."

In our upstairs bathroom, which is kind of neat and old-fashioned with little black and white octagonal tiles on the floor and a bathtub with claw feet, there's a big wicker basket next to the toilet, the kind of basket most people use for plants. Ours is filled with *Gourmet* magazines and playscripts.

My own bathroom reading runs more to history books, the fatter the better. I'm not very discriminating. I read anything that's history, any period, any country, just as long as it's about the past. I've read about the Russian Revolution, the sixties in the United States, medicine in the Middle Ages, and the bloody jostling for power of the English royal families. "You're a little too haphazard in your reading," Totie Golden, my history teacher, says. She's right. One of these days I'll settle down and start at the beginning (if I can figure out where that is—it all depends on your point of view), get serious and systematic. Meanwhile, I raid the library shelves. The way I see it, even with some of the real horrendo things that happened to people, like the rack torture and legs being amputated without anesthesia, the past had to be better than where we are now, with all the pollution and chemical junk and the Big Bang hanging over our heads. I think I could be happy going back to live anywhere, anytime, in the past.

Sometimes I try to get my uncle to read something besides recipes, plays, and eyeglass magazines. "Don't have the time, Pete," he says. Maybe, and maybe he's just stubborn, just doesn't want to do anything I suggest. He always comes across sort of mild and sweet, but I notice that things in the house go pretty much the way he wants them to.

Another thing he never does is eat the food I make. "Gene, want to taste something fantastic?" I stirred the Sloppy Joe I was cooking. It smelled authentic—School Cafeteria a la Mode.

My uncle looked into the pot. "No thanks."

"Not so fast." I went after him with the spoon. "Come on. Taste!"

"Pete, that spoon is dripping all over."

"Taste it and it won't drip." He eyed me. I eyed him back. I'd been in a rotten mood for days. Was it unreasonable to think that Laura and Hal, also known as my parents, could have figured out a way to mail me a letter so it would reach me by my birthday? Or weren't they going to write me a birthday letter this year? Maybe they'd forgotten the big date, or figured at sixteen I should forget about things like birthday letters and presents.

"A little bite of my food won't kill you, Gene."

13

"Martha and I are going to try out that new Japanese restaurant." He looked at his watch. "She'll be here in half an hour."

"Listen, I eat your slop—excuse me, your creations—all the time, so how about a little reciprocity?"

"Is it my imagination, or have you become difficult since you hit sixteen?"

"You're jumping the gun. Four more days. Right now I'm still just a difficult fifteen-year-old. And you said the same thing last year on my birthday."

"Come on, Pete, I'm sure I didn't."

"You'd better watch it, Uncle Gene. Repetition is one of the seven danger signs of creeping old age. How old are you anyway, Gene?"

"What difference does that make?"

I knew he'd say that. Gene is sensitive about his age and his looks. Martha says all actors are like that. I'd just been baiting him, being obnoxious, but all of a sudden I went into one of my maniac rages. I threw down the spoon. "Why can't you just answer the goddamn question?"

As usual when I acted like a psycho, Gene got very calm. Didn't say a word. Just picked up the spoon, wiped the floor, and went upstairs, removing himself from the vicinity of the mad dog. I foamed at the mouth for a few more minutes, throwing things around. Then I sat down at the kitchen table with the pot of Sloppy Joe.

What a pig I was, taking out my lousy feelings on Gene. He was good, he was fair, he didn't make unjust demands on me. (Thank you, Uncle Gene.) I had money in my pocket, clothes on my back. (Thank you, Uncle Gene.) He didn't treat me like a kid or a ward or a dependent. (Thank you, Uncle Gene.)

He came back downstairs, dressed for his date with Martha: ruffled white shirt, gold cufflinks, and his old, gold Bulova watch. He took the water bottle from the refrigerator and poured a glass of water. "Sorry," I mumbled, and dumped the Sloppy Joe into the garbage as a peace offering.

Gene looked at me over the rim of the glass. "Am I wrong, or was that quite a little blowup over nothing?" He sipped his water and spoke slowly. "We've been living together nearly eight years, Pete. "Seems like we should have things worked out enough by now, so if something's on your mind—"

"I just got mad."

"You often just get mad."

"I don't mean to. It just happens."

"Do you think you could try not to let it happen?"

"I don't know. Maybe." I actually don't think there's anything I can do about it. I don't plan to go crazy, it just hits me. Things get to me, and va-voom!

Gene sat down across from me and sighed. He has a whole repertoire of magnificent sighs. I guess they come in handy on the stage. Sometimes all he does is sigh, and that gets across his point. This was a sigh that told me a story was coming.

"Eight years ago, Pete, I had a very strange phone call. A total stranger called me and said, 'I have something to tell you. Please trust me. Your sister and her husband are in trouble, something very bad has happened, unexpected, and they have to drop out of sight for a while. Can you take their little boy until things calm down?' I wasn't asked to think it over and I didn't need to. I reacted instinctively, I guess anyone would in the situation . . . Pete, are you listening?"

"Yes."

"Your eyes are closed."

"They are?" I sat up. "I heard every word you said, Gene. Go on." Even though I'd heard all this in one

15

form or another before, I never minded hearing it again. "So you got this phone call and then—"

" 'Well,' I said, 'yes, I'll take the boy.' I hung up. And then I got a reaction. My God, what is this? What have I done? I haven't seen Laura in years, she's not even my full sister! I thought I was mad. What did I know about little boys? As for you, we'd never even met. I'd had pictures of you from Laura now and then, and that was it."

"So why didn't you call back and say, 'Sorry, folks, deal's off'?"

"Lots of reasons. She *is* my sister. Just because we had different fathers—no, the half sister thought was absolutely mindless panic." He tipped back in his chair. "Besides, I didn't have the option of calling my mysterious caller back. I said yes, he hung up, and it wasn't till hours later that I realized I didn't have a name, I didn't have a number, I didn't have a clue! What sort of trouble were Laura and Hal in? Well, actually, it didn't take too much to figure out it had to be something political."

"Did that bother you?" I asked. Gene is probably the most *un*political person in the world. If he didn't have to go to an office every day to make bucks, he'd be content to spend his life thinking about nothing but plays and food.

"Maybe it worried me a little. I knew the two of them had been marching and shouting and demonstrating against the bomb and the military for years. Maybe I'd been half-expecting Laura to get into trouble. Once she did, do you remember that?"

"When? What kind of trouble?"

"Oh, she was in some sort of demonstration—the military was deploying one of those missiles, and she climbed a fence and got herself arrested with a bunch of other women. I sent your father bail money for her. She spent two nights in jail and then, luck-

16

ily, the charges were dismissed. I didn't keep up with their activities. Once in a while, I'd read something in the paper or Laura would write me a letter and say, 'Well, we just threw blood on the Pentagon,' something like that. You know they were always doing things—draping the flag of that organization of theirs on the Statue of Liberty or lying down in front of cars going to air bases—I don't know, I never thought it meant that much, but it was their whole life. Anyway, what I remember thinking after that phone call was that this time they must have done something pretty serious. Such as? I didn't know—maybe destroyed government property, bashed up some military vehicle—I just didn't know. My imagination didn't take me any farther than that. All the things they'd ever done over the years, they'd been pretty legal, protected by the First Amendment, or whatever. Still, I couldn't understand—why go into hiding? For a lot of these people, publicity is really what they want."

"Wait a minute, wait a minute," I said. "You make it sound so cynical, as if everything they do is for publicity. That's dead wrong! They have ideals, they have principles, they don't do these things for any selfish gain."

"Cool down," my uncle said. "You misunderstand me. What I meant is that they need media attention so they can make their statements. Did you notice the article in the newspaper yesterday about the seven Quakers who broke into a draft board office to protest our military policy? They hung around for two hours waiting for someone to come along and arrest them. That was the sort of thing Laura and Hal would have done." He thumped down his chair. "Then that day, or maybe it was the next morning, I don't remember which, I read in the newspaper about the explosion in Femmer Lab. And I started putting two and two together. Did you know right away? You were such a little kid, but—"

"Not that little, Gene. Laura and Hal never treated me like a baby. I knew they were going to do something important, but they were coming back. That was the plan. Then I heard on the radio . . . what happened . . . and those people—" I broke off. I didn't want to talk about the Femmer Lab thing.

"Go on with your story, Gene," I said. "So you got this phone call. And then you got cold feet. What next? I arrive with Uncle Marti, right?"

"I wonder what his real name was. Did you know?"

"I just knew him as Uncle Marti. Does it matter?"

"I suppose not. It's just—sometimes I think back to that phone conversation and I have to laugh. Would I take care of you for 'a little while,' he said. That, to me, at that moment meant a week, at the outside a month. What did I know about taking care of a child? I didn't have much time to prepare, I'll tell you that. Twenty four hours later, there you were, delivered to me in the middle of the night. A nephew package, complete with roped suitcase and two grocery bags of toys, special delivery from my little sister, Laura. I might have lost my head if I'd known that 'little while' was going to turn into eight years."

"Or what a maniac you were bringing into your house."

"Some maniac. Holding on for dear life to that stuffed cat or whatever it was—"

"Dog," I said. "Emory Doghead Dog . . . You came to the door in pink pajamas."

"I never had pink pajamas."

Maybe he was right. I don't have that many clear memories of the past—why should I remember that night any better than anything else? The year I was thirteen, I started spending every spare moment in

18

the library reading about my parents, going through years of *Readers Guides'* and the *New York Times Index;* looking under AWE, Bombing, Connors, Radical Left, Revolution, Underground. I thought I knew a lot about my parents, but I came up with all sorts of stuff—articles, pictures, editorials—more stuff than I'd ever imagined had been written about them.

Now it bothers me quite a lot that I'm not sure about the memories I have. Those pictures I tote around in my mind—aren't a lot of them actually from newspapers and magazines? Laura in her mortarboard. Hal holding up a mammoth sign. Laura reaching with a frantic smile for Hal being pulled away by two policemen. Public parents, public pictures. Where are the private pictures, the memories, the images, the flashes of light from the past that are mine alone?

Riding Hal's shoulders through a mass of people . . . up there above everyone else, clutching his hair, laughing because I was Prince of the Hill on top of my daddy . . . and all the banners waving and people singing . . . "We will not, we will not, we will not be MOVED. Just like a tre-eee standing by the wa-aa-ter, we will not be moved . . ."

Marching next to my mother in front of the White House with a sign as big as me hung across my chest . . . MR. PRESIDENT, I AM 5 YEARS OLD AND I WANT TO LIVE. NO MORE NUCLEAR WEAPONS.

I remember those things, I'm sure I do. And more— Hal being torn off a pole by the police . . . and mounted policemen riding toward us, the horses' legs as tall as the sky . . . and running with Laura, who held my hand so hard I thought our hands would melt together, one hand forever.

I say I'm sure, and then I'm not sure. Are these actual memories of my own—or are they movie and TV clips? I don't have my parents. I don't have my name. Is it too much to ask for my own memories?

"Pink pajamas," I repeated stubbornly. "You were wearing pink pajamas, and the way I was feeling, dazed out, I thought you were a big pink rabbit. Don't laugh. I did. Alice-in-Wonderland time."

"No pink pajamas," Gene said. "Never."

When the two of us knock heads, we usually don't get anywhere but mad. Fortunately, Martha came in just then.

"Hi, guys." She threw off her shawl, tossed it on the table. She has a way of doing things that makes you aware of how big she is. I don't mean she's gigantic, but for a woman she's pretty big, tall and broad-shouldered—as big as Gene and quite a bit bigger than I am. What's odd is that her voice is high and little, almost like a kid's.

She has her own way of dressing, too. Tonight she was wearing her bright red and black Peruvian shawl, a faded green cotton skirt, and Mexican sandals that squeaked. Nothing matched, yet everything seemed right. That was Martha.

"You look great," I said. "Like something out of the fifties."

"I hope you mean the decade, not my age."

I laughed. There is definitely something about her that gets to me.

"Oh, what a gorgeous night out there. Warm! Plus—would you believe—stars! More like June than March." She kissed Gene on the mouth, ruffled my hair and hugged me.

Martha's a very physical person, which is good, because Gene and I are both sort of inhibited about

20

hugging and kissing. I really like Martha as a friend, but I also have a lot of attraction to her. I read that in some countries, like France, older women take young guys as their lovers and teach them all about sex. I instantly thought of Martha and me. Of course it could never happen because of her and Gene, but that doesn't stop me from having wild fantasies. One favorite is where Gene has a heart attack or a broken leg—something serious but not fatal—that lands him in the hospital for quite a while. As a good friend of the family, Martha moves into our place to help me out . . . and we get friendlier and friendlier . . . and friendlier.

Actually, Martha's never stayed overnight at our house, although Gene fairly often stays over at her place. Do they think I don't know what goes on? Or do they just like doing it without me around?

"What are you two chewing over?" Martha said.

Gene and I exchanged a quick look. That was it. Differences forgotten. The important thing was, no talking about the past in front of Martha. She didn't know anything about it.

"Pete made a foul pot of something for supper tonight," Gene said, "and we got into a little hassle over it."

"Look, Unc, I threw it out. That ought to satisfy you."

"*You* threw out food?" Martha said. "It must have been incredibly raunchy, Pete. I've seen you eat some very questionable mixes."

"You see," Gene said, "even Martha, who thinks you do no wrong, doesn't like the messes you brew in the kitchen."

"Messes!" I howled. I clutched my heart, and Gene rolled his eyes at my flamboyance. We were like a comedy team or two magicians, distracting Martha so she wouldn't ask any more questions.

From the Manila Envelope

Explosion Damages Lab
Fire Chief Says No Theories Yet

An explosion of unknown origin ripped through the Femmer Laboratory in the Franklin Butler Building at Beecham University last night sometime past midnight, causing extensive damage and endangering adjoining buildings. While firemen battled the three-alarm blaze, police threw up a cordon to hold off the crowds of curious students who converged on the scene, some of them in nightclothes. One young man was there with a tennis racket. He explained, "The courts are so crowded that the only time I can get on them is after midnight. But this is more fun than a tennis game." An almost festive air held sway. A green truck with "GrubStake" painted on it did a brisk business in hot dogs, soda, and French fries. Between bites of food, students called encouragement to the firemen, who went about their business without responding.

Fire Chief Paul Marshallo said he did not yet have any theories about the origin of the explosion. "It could have been somebody careless with cigarettes and some of those chemicals they've got there," he said. "It could have been arson. It could have been anything. We're investigating. It might be arson. We'll investigate the possibility of arson. This lab was doing pretty important research. Government stuff. But I don't want to say anything firm yet. We have to investigate all possibilities and keep an open mind."

Three

When Martha and Gene left, I watched from the living room window as they got into Martha's VW bug. I have Martha's promise that if she ever sells the bug, I get first dibs. Originally it was a nice light green, but now one fender's a mottled brown and the other's red. The engine is still great, though. We, or Gene really, have a big dignified Volvo, but it was at the dealer's for brake work. It's ten years old and always at the dealer's for something or other. Considering that Gene walks to and from his office and we don't have our own garage and can't park in front of the house for more than an hour without hitting the meter, the V is nothing but a big expensive nuisance, but Gene loves it and doesn't care.

He's been trying to get the city to zone our block for unlimited day parking for years, but it's a losing battle. We live in the only remaining private house downtown, and the land developers, who are all tight with City Hall, would love to drive us out and get their hands on our place. Not for the house—they wouldn't care about that at all. It's limestone and it was originally a farmhouse. Long before I came to live with him, Gene had reworked the whole house, pulling down walls to make fewer but bigger rooms, uncovering the old fireplaces, and tearing up layers

23

of cruddy linoleum to get to the original wide, pine plank floors. The house is really his baby. He tried for a long time to have it declared a historic building. He lost that battle, too.

Since we live downtown in the middle of stores and offices, some nights it's as quiet as the country. This was one of the country nights. That is, until Martha pulled away from the curb. She likes to say that in another life she wasn't an artist, she was a racing car driver. I watched out the front window as she roared down the street.

A moment later, another car pulled away from the curb. Coincidence? That made the most sense—but not to me. I jerked open the front door and ran down the stone walk. Where had the car been parked? Had someone been watching the house? My stomach lurched, a hand in there grabbing and squeezing. I was lucky, half lucky—I raced down the street, caught sight of the car just before it turned the corner. I got the first three letters of the license plate. Not good, but enough for an entry.

In my room, I filed the information under NOTED. "AAR . . . B1. 4 dr F. new, fllwd G&M in bug." I kept my sightings in an ordinary green school notebook divided into two sections, DEFINITE and NOTED. Every time I made an entry, I checked and cross-checked to see if that particular car had ever turned up before. Now and then, it happened.

I was still flipping through the pages and brooding over the car that had (might have?) followed Gene and Martha, when the phone rang in the kitchen. The hand grabbed me in the belly again. I shoved the notebook into my desk. The phone kept ringing.

"I'm coming," I yelled as I went downstairs.

"Hi, Peter."

"Deirdre!" I hitched myself onto the counter.

24

"How'd you know it was me, Peter?" She pronounced it *Peet-ah*.

"I ought to know your voice by now, Dee."

"That's true, I always recognize your smashing voice when you call us, luv." Deirdre is one of my friend Drew's sisters. For about two years, she's been crazy for anything English. She listens only to English rock groups, says "smashing" as often as possible, and reads everything written on Princess Di. "No one else sounds like you, old chap, but I didn't know *I* had such a distinctive voice."

"Bloody modest of you, luv."

"You're teasing me, Pete!" she said, suddenly sounding like the old Deirdre.

I've known Deirdre almost as long as I've known Drew. She, Dawn, Drew, and I used to play kickball and King of the Hill together. Deirdre's a year older than I am, Dawn's a year younger. It was always Deirdre I was interested in. Sometimes we used to go off by ourselves to talk. I was a fairly horny little kid even in elementary school, and I spent a lot of time praying for Deirdre to be overcome by passion for me. All she ever did, though, was complain about her mother's favoring Drew over her and Dawn. Once, when I tried to kiss her, she just laughed.

"Where's Drew?" I said now.

"Oh, he and Mummy went out to look at stuff for the shop. Some bloody old antique dining room set. I called to ask when you're coming over, Peter. We blokes haven't seen you in a huge while. Come on over and have supper with us one of these nights."

"If you promise to sit next to me."

"Oh, my, aren't you growing up, though."

"I've been this way for years, luv. Remember when I tried to kiss you?"

"Hmmm. Can't say that I do, Peet-ah. Don't tell me about it! I always thought you were the nicest

25

boy I knew. I don't want to get all disillusioned about you."

We fooled around like that for a while. All the time, in the back of my mind, I wondered if anyone was listening to our conversation. I have this clear picture in my head of a man in a cellar. I can't see his face, but I know he's wearing earphones and chain-smoking. Next to him there's a tape deck, turning and turning, recording all our thousands of conversations. Martha to Gene. Gene to me. Me to Drew. Nothing exciting, nothing unusual, but the man doesn't care. He's patient, the way a hunter has to be patient. He's waiting. Waiting for me or Gene to forget, to make one unguarded comment, one indiscreet remark. That's all he would need. Actually, in this age of electronic miracles, I guess tapping phones is done a lot more easily than sticking some poor agent into a damp cellar. But somebody has to listen to the stuff, don't they? It might as well be my faceless man in the cellar.

Four

"Don't you get it?" I said, handing Drew the Koren cartoon. I hated that anxious note in my voice. What did it matter if Drew got it or not? When was I going to stop being so damn dependent on his good opinion?

It was lunchtime and we were outside, sharing Winston High's somewhat soggy lawn with about two thousand other students playing killer Frisbee, eating, and looking for places to make out or smoke. Winston High is one of those windowless wonders. As soon as the snow melts, the cafeteria is deserted. Even in the middle of winter, there are diehards who go outside and sit in snowdrifts to eat their lunches.

Drew pulled at his lower lip as he studied the cartoon. I'd cut it out of an old *New Yorker* magazine that had been hanging around my uncle's office. I practically worshipped Koren as a true genius. His cartoons were tacked up all over my bedroom walls. This one showed four typical shaggy Koren animal-people—or people-animals, take your choice—with their fuzzy clothes and anteater snouts, sitting around a fire in a living room. They were all holding wineglasses and while the other three smiled benignly on her, one of the female shaggy types said, "I love to be alive. It's fun."

"You really think that's funny?" Drew said, handing back the cartoon. " 'I love to be alive, it's fun'? I don't get it. I mean, that's pretty obvious."

"That's the point. It's so obvious and banal and understated. That's what makes it funny."

Drew slung an arm over my shoulder. "I'll take your word for it. Wendy Varner called me last night. You should have heard her. You should have heard the things she said."

"Quit slobbering on my neck. Don't you ever think about anything except girls?"

"Do you?"

"Now and then, now and then. Anyway, I thought you were in love with Joanie."

"I am."

"So what's this Wendy Varner stuff?"

"She called me. What was I supposed to do? Hang up on her?"

"Dear Drew," a girl had written him in third grade, the year he and I had become friends, "I love you." And ever since, girls had been slipping notes into his desk, his books, and his locker, one way or another always leaving the same message. "Dear Drew, I love you."

It was truly depressing to think about his endless string of girl friends. As far as girls went, he was world-class and I was no-class. I could count my lifetime record for girlfriends on the fingers of one finger. Barbara Hart, who not only let me kiss her behind Wood Street Elementary School but also, in exchange for a mere bag of marbles, showed me a patch of her bare stomach, *including belly button.* Hot stuff for fifth grade. However, that moment of glory was far behind me. A long drought since then.

I'd always liked girls. It didn't come on me suddenly, ta ta! ta ta!, big burst of adolescent frenzy. What had changed was how much I liked girls and how much it bothered me that there wasn't a girl in sight who liked me back.

I fingered the two hairs on my chin. Drew had a mustache already. "Remember Barbara Hart?"

"Fifth grade," Drew said. "All Hart. What brought her to mind?"

"Did I ever tell you I had a hot romance going with her?"

"Who didn't?" Drew said, chewing on a twig. "When she moved away, she had the biggest marble collection in Wood Street School."

I sat up. "You're just saying that to drive me crazy."

"Ah, Pete! For a smart guy— Did you think you were the only one? I bet she gave you the old belly-button treatment, too. Right? Right? Six marbles?"

"You only had to give her six? A whole bag of my best marbles."

"Now *that's* funny!"

I punched him on the arm. "The hell it is."

He grinned and gave me a stinging slap on the cheek. "Sure you want to start this, Pete?"

"I'll take you."

"It'll be the first time." Another slap.

We had met eight years ago on my first day in Wood Street Elementary School third grade. I had lived with my uncle for about two weeks by then, spending my days playing around his office. In school, in a hushed sorrowful voice, he told the principal that I had always been taught at home by my parents, who had recently died and left him to be my guardian. Things, he said, were still chaotic, and he didn't have the family documents yet.

Miss Simpson, the third-grade teacher, put me in the seat next to Drew. Greenwood, Gregoretti. Later that day, she told me I did fine work and that maybe

29

I could help Drew with his reading. Then she asked me what Pax was short for.

"It means peace."

"Well . . . yes. Peace. I thought maybe it was a family name?"

I shook my head no and then yes, and she let me go. I reported this conversation to my uncle at suppertime.

"I guess we didn't think of everything," he said. By then we both knew that I would be staying with him longer than a few days or a month. Word had come to him, again through an anonymous phone call, that it would be for a year, at least. After that call, the decision had been made for me to enroll in school under Gene's name. He said, "Maybe it would be a good idea to change your first name, too. Not too much, hmmm? How does Pete sound to you?"

"Okay."

In school, I told Miss Simpson that Pax was just a nickname and she should call me Pete. No one ever remembered that for one day I had been Pax—except me. For months, I was anxious about my name, afraid I'd forget, not respond when the teacher called on me. And I was constantly on guard, waiting for some kid or teacher to come up and say, *Hey! How come you changed your name?* Just the thought of it turned me damp and hot with anxiety. I figured out what I'd say. At home, I wrote it down and I memorized it. *I didn't change my name! I told you, that was just a family name, sort of a nickname. My name is Pete!* I practiced saying it to my mirror and to Emory Doghead Dog. But inside me, I knew that, no matter what I said, they wouldn't believe me, that something in my voice or my face would give me away.

After about six months of being Pete Greenwood, it began to seem almost like my real name. Sometimes I even wrote it on my school papers without first reminding myself, You're Pete Greenwood. I had taken to writing very carefully, very slowly, to give myself time to remember. But even after I began writing "Pete Greenwood" automatically on top of my school papers, I never got over my fear that someone would know or guess the truth about me.

I worried the most about Drew, because we were together so much. It was Drew who decided we were going to be friends. Every morning, wearing a Yankee tee-shirt and tossing a baseball, he waited for me on the corner of Brighton and Western avenues near the school. He must have worn something else at times—a jacket, a sweater—but what I remember is that Yankee tee-shirt and his blue baseball cap. Even then, when we were only eight years old, he was built like a tree. He was solid. And even then, despite my nearly constant underground anxiety, I knew that I would always know where I stood with Drew. There were no surprises, no shadows, nothing hiding behind his rosy-faced friendliness but friendliness. Knowing that Drew would be there on that corner made it a lot easier for me to get out of bed every morning in this strange new world, without my parents and without my own name.

"Got you!" Drew said now, grabbing me in a bear hug. I managed to hook a foot behind his ankle and we both went down, but with Drew on top.

"Say uncle, Pete."

"Like hell."

"Uncle, Pete!"

I pounded him. He grabbed my hands and held them easily in his two big paws. My helplessness brought something sour into my throat. I thrashed around. "Get the hell off me, Gregoretti."

He didn't move, grinned wider, sat there big and superior. *I love you, Drew,* the girls said, but never

31

had one said it to me. I stopped struggling and just lay there and felt depressed about everything. Girls . . . and what I knew about me and my parents that no one else knew . . . and how it set me apart . . . made me different from everyone else. Secretly different.

On some level, I was always pretending, always playing a role. See me be Pete-the-normal-average-American-boy. My differentness wasn't something I could point to or talk about. It wasn't like the comedian I'd seen on TV, a woman who had cerebral palsy and made you laugh about things you always thought you had to be so secret and sober about. One of her routines was, "Hi, I'm Jill, I have cerebral palsy. What's your problem?"

Hi, I'm Pete-Pax, I have parents hiding from the law. What's your problem?

"Hey, bozo, say uncle."

"Forget it."

"Stubborn little runt, aren't you?"

I forced a grin as big as his. It was unworthy of me to be depressed. Hal and Laura were the special people. Heroes, doing the deeds that would save humanity. In a flash I saw them bestriding the world like the ancient gods and heroes, my mother an Amazon, my father a Colossus. Next to them, all others were puny. I forced the smile to be proud . . . my mouth stretched . . . Hal . . . Laura . . . you're mine, my parents . . . someday everyone will know. . . .

My forehead broke out in a sweat. Everyone will know. Just thinking it was like a door opening. The other thoughts came sweeping in through that open door. *Those people . . . shouldn't have been there . . . bodies . . . why did they . . . bodies . . . and two peo-*

ple . . . No. No! *No.* Push it away, don't think it, don't let it be there in your head.

I closed my eyes, blanked out. Nothing there. No thoughts, no bad thoughts, nothing . . . nothing.

"Hey, you playing dead?" Drew lightly slapped me on the face.

I kept my eyes closed.

Nothing . . . nothing . . . nothing . . . my mind all dark and empty, blank . . .

The bell rang. "Saved by the bell," Drew said, getting up. "Next time, Pete, you say uncle twice to make up for it."

I stood up, stretched, yawned and yawned and yawned. I was suddenly exhausted. It was an effort for me to lope along with Drew toward school, an effort to say in as casual a voice as his, "You could have sat on me till Christmas and I wouldn't have said it."

From the Manila Envelope

Couple, Eight-Year-Old Son Missing

Following information given them by unnamed sources, FBI agents tonight searched the apartment of Harold (Hal) and Laura Connors, who are wanted for questioning in the Femmer Laboratory bombing. The couple, who has been active in a movement known as Air, Water, Earth (AWE), have not been seen for over a week. The FBI has refused to release any information on the missing couple and their child.

When questioned, neighbors described the couple as "lovely people," "so gentle," "devoted to their little boy." One neighbor in their modest apartment building, Mrs. Rita Ritzo, cried as she talked about the family. "I'm all alone. I lost my husband last year. I baby-sat for the boy now and then, and they were wonderful to me. One Sunday they took me along when they had a picnic. I can't believe what they're saying on the TV and in the newspapers."

Five

Ordinarily, if I don't have anything else to do after school, I go to Gene's office. There's always work there for me—sweeping floors or stuffing envelopes or making a run to the post office for stamps. Whatever, I do it. But the day before my birthday, I just didn't feel like the office. Still no letter from my parents. Okay, that's cool. Probably Gene would give me a check—that is, if he remembered the big day. I decided not to expect anything, then I couldn't be disappointed. Very sensible, but I was a little depressed, anyway.

Looking for some conversation, I stopped in to see Martha in her corner store. For once she was busy. She does charcoal and pastel portraits for ten dollars a shot. People think she must be rolling in dough at that rate, but what they don't understand is how few people are willing to part with a tenner for a portrait of little Janie or Johnny.

She was at work on a charcoal of a little girl with big chipmunk teeth. This kid couldn't keep all of her still for more than two seconds. Her mother kept saying, "Let the lady draw your picture! Danielle! Don't wriggle!"

Danielle twitched, fidgeted, sighed, tapped her feet, and twiddled her fingers. "Hey, Danielle," I said, "watch this." I flapped my hands in my ears and crossed my eyes. Danielle looked bored.

"Good try," Martha said.

Christmas is Martha's big season. The rest of the year she does what she calls "eking." Gene calls her apartment a little hole in the wall, but Martha always has it filled with big bunches of dried grasses and lots of her own watercolors of barns and streams in autumn, so actually you don't pay much attention to how dark and small it is. And to listen to her talk about shopping in secondhand stores, you'd think it was a rare privilege for her *not* to be able to afford new things. "Old clothes have cachet," she says. "They've been broken in, softened, they're not hard and garish like so many new things."

Sometimes I feel guilty because Martha has so little money, while I don't have any money worries at all (thank you, Uncle Gene), but I don't see what I can do about making things any different for her. Well, actually that ties right into one of my fantasies, too.

This one starts with me as the rising young lawyer who defends a case (brilliantly, for something important like free speech) up to the Supreme Court. My eloquence makes me famous, brings me tons of clients. I get rich and have more money than I know what to do with. I tell Martha I won't allow her to waste her talents for another moment on ten-dollar charcoal sketches of squirmy brats. She's going to have a real studio, with northern light, all the expensive oils she wants, canvases, models, the whole works. And what do I want in return? Nothing! Just the satisfaction of knowing I've helped her. But Martha is so impressed by my noble unselfishness, she falls in love with me and begs me to make love to her. Which I do, after only a little hesitation. (Tough luck, Uncle Gene.)

When I left Martha, it had started to rain, a kind of warm spring rain. I stopped in the Nut Shoppe to buy a bag of hot peanuts. A girl was sitting on a high stool behind the counter at the back of the store. I say that so casually, but seeing her I thought—*Oh!*

Her hair was pulled back clean from a high shining forehead with a tortoiseshell band. She had a little round chin and tiny gold birds pinned into her ears. She was reading a book and wore a blue and white checked smock with the sleeves rolled up to the elbow. That smock was all wrong. The smock was Peasant. The girl was Princess. She was beautiful, but it was something else that drew me to her. Something about her, something different—I didn't know what. Not the princess thing. No, quite the contrary—princesses scared me, and in one way, so did she. Yet the moment I saw her, something changed for me. I had to know her.

She looked up, a brief cool glance, clicked her tongue as if I were an annoyance instead of a customer, put a marker in her book, closed it, and slid off the stool. All very deliberate. No hurry. The aliens had captured her, dropped her into this mundane peanut-selling shop and wouldn't let her leave. But she knew (and now I knew) she was of royal blood.

"May I help you?" she said.

"Peanuts . . . I mean, a pound—hot—please, thank you." I all but bent from the waist. I paid for the peanuts and walked over to Gene's office, thinking about the girl and going *ohhh, ohhh, ohhh* to myself.

As soon as I walked in, Janice Silk, my uncle's receptionist, crooked her finger at me. Silky's worked for Gene as long as I can remember. Once, on some anniversary or other, Gene said she was just like a member of the family, but it's not true. Silky has her own family, two sons and two daughters, Gene and I

37

have each other, and none of us ever get together outside the office.

"Am I glad to see you," Silky said, glancing at the couple in the waiting room. "The lab needs a good cleaning. Your uncle was wondering where you were. He's in room two with a patient."

The door to room two was open. "Now look at the center of this ruler I'm holding across my nose," Gene was saying to the man in the chair. He flashed a light into the man's eyes. "Fine, fine, *very* good." Gene always sounds tremendously encouraging as he puts his patients through the routine refractions, as if they're passing a difficult test. I waved to him, made sweeping motions, and pointed toward the lab.

I got out the cleaning stuff and then just stood there daydreaming. Stop thinking about the Peanut Princess. Discipline the mind. Concentrate on important things, like sweeping. Okay, I'm not thinking about her anymore. (Then why am I thinking about her?)

I leaned on the broom. I had to see her again. The only question was, when? I could act cool (SIR SKINNY LEGS DECIDES TO MAKE PEANUT PRINCESS WAIT FOR HER SECOND ELECTRIFYING GLIMPSE OF HIS INCREDIBLE PRESENCE) and not go there for several days. Good move, but what if, in the meantime, she met another guy, quit the job, or moved away? Obviously, I should act fast. Go back tomorrow. However, in order not to be totally obvious about my interest in her, this time I'd buy pistachios. And while she was weighing and bagging them, I'd impress the hell out of her. (How was I going to do that? The same way I'd knocked her socks off today with my wit and charm? *Uhhh, a pound of peanuts . . . uhhh, hot . . . uhhh, thank you.* What would I do for an encore—show her my legs?)

I pushed the broom around the floor. Why so humble? The Princess and the Peasant! Pete, that is disgusting. Listen up: The Princess is not your type (since when did I have a type?), she wears too much makeup (now I'm an expert on makeup?), and has serious character defects—aloof, cold. (Was I sure about that? What if she was just shy?) She *was* pretty—I'd give her that. (Generous of me. She was actually gorgeous and probably had truckloads of guys following her every step.)

I swept up the dust and dropped it into the wastebasket. How to make her notice me? How not to be just another one of the drooling mob panting after her?

"Everything okay, Pete?" Gene said, passing by. Typically, he had a mild, worried expression, something like a bighorn sheep, an expression that at certain times could vastly irritate me.

"Everything's terrific, Uncle G," I called after him. I pinched my nose and honked, "My dear Miss Nut Shoppe, I have admired you from afar, but now the time has come to speak out."

All through supper I thought about the girl. All evening when I was supposedly studying I thought about her, and lots and lots when I was in bed. First thing in the morning I thought about her and all day in school. Was the Peanut Princess really that four-star special? Or was I doing a number on myself so I wouldn't have to think how today was my birthday and how I hadn't heard from Laura and Hal?

Happy birthday to me, happy birthday to me, happy birthday, Pete Pax, happy birthday to me. Okay, I was feeling sorry for myself. Poor little neglected birthday boy. I actually felt too sorry for me to even want to go see the Peanut Princess. What for? So she could snub me? I felt so sorry for me that instead of running the couple of miles downtown from school, which always made me feel more athletic than I am, I ate my way home. I stopped in every little grocery and fast-food place I passed. I had:

1. A Giant Benny Burger.

2. Two cones of McDonald's French fries.

3. Three fat House of Pancakes blueberry pancakes.

4. A triple-dip black and white soft ice cream coated with chocolate and sprinkles (fifty cents extra).

5. A large bag of corn chips, a large bag of potato chips, two coconut candy bars, and three soft drinks.

Happy birthday to me.

Six

Martha rapped on my door. "Pete, we're going to have supper."

"I'm not hungry." I was lying on my bed, me and my birthday bellyache.

"Up, boy. Gene's been working for hours on one of his famous gourmet productions."

I waved her away.

"What can I do to change your mind?"

"Nothing," I said.

She left, but a few minutes later she was back again holding a huge white frosted cake. "Surprise! You are surprised, aren't you? I told Gene you didn't realize what was going on. We're having a little party for you. This is my contribution."

"You baked it?"

"Did you ever hear of me baking anything? This is an On the Rise Bakery special. I told them seventeen candles. One for each year and one to grow on. That's the way we always did it back home." She slapped my hand away from the frosting. "Come on, comb your hair, tuck in your shirt, and come down. And don't forget I only bought this cake, but Gene's been working on this dinner for hours."

The dining room table was set with Gene's best

stuff. It looked like something out of a magazine. There were even flowers in the middle.

Gene came in from the kitchen carrying the soup tureen in two hands. He was wearing his long blue linen chef's apron. Too bad I wasn't hungry. Besides the bouillabaisse, there was asparagus, which I'm a fiend for, especially the way Gene cooks it, bright green and crisp. He has a special asparagus pot and, for serving, a special oval, pale green asparagus plate.

"The bouillabaisse is *won*derful," Martha said. "You've outdone yourself, Gene." She kicked me under the table.

"For fish soup, not half half bad, Uncle G."

"High praise. Is that all you're going to eat?"

"Actually, like I told Martha, I'm not all that hungry. I had a little something on the way home."

"What sort of little something?"

I didn't want to give Gene a heart attack, so I said, "An ice cream cone."

"That doesn't sound like so much."

"Triple-dip."

"Too bad you didn't save your appetite. Didn't you figure out I'd be making you a dinner? I do it every year."

"I forgot," I said. "Anyway," I added as a diversion, "I thought I was getting a sore throat."

Gene put down the pepper mill. "What does ice cream have to do with a sore throat?"

"Uncle G! It's a well-known cure for sore throats."

Besides the soup and asparagus, there was hot garlicky French bread and a cheese board with Brie and Camembert, all things I really like, but I couldn't stuff in another anything. I did drink a glass of wine, though.

The cake was last. "Make a wish, Pete," Martha said.

"I'm getting kind of big for that."

"Oh, you're never too old to wish," Martha said. "I do it every year."

"Okay." I wished and blew out the candles.

"What'd you wish for?" Gene asked.

"It's going to come true because he blew them all out, but he can't tell," Martha said, "or he'll jinx it." She pushed back her chair. "Cut me a big slice, Pete, I'm really into celebrating your birthday." She went into the kitchen.

I cut the cake, thinking that for eight years I'd always had the same wish—for my parents to return. But Martha was wrong, my wish wasn't going to come true. Why this year and not last year? Why not next year? Or the year after?

Martha came back with her arms full of packages. "Happy birthday, Pete, from Gene and me."

"Wow," I said like a little kid. "Where'd you hide all this stuff?"

"Us to know and you to wonder."

"In Martha's apartment," Gene said.

"Gene! You gave it away." She grabbed his shoulders and shook him.

I started opening the packages. From Gene, socks, tee-shirts, underwear, and a Norwegian ski sweater. "I know it's not the season," he said, "but it'll keep till next winter." There were also two tens folded into a brand-new wallet. And from Martha, a historical atlas, which I'd been wanting, and a Honey in the Rock poster.

I kept saying, "Thank you, thank you."

"You're most welcome," Martha said and gave me a terrific kiss, right on the mouth. "Now you two hug each other," she ordered. Gene and I sort of pawed each other on the shoulder, then we shook hands.

After that the party went on for another hour or so and I drank a couple more glasses of wine. I knew I

43

was drunk, or high anyway, when I noticed that I was feeling extremely happy.

"Happiness is not my long suit," I said to Martha. "I am not often happy." It seemed immensely profound, but Martha laughed.

"Of course you're happy. Sixteen is the best time of life."

"When I was sixteen," Gene said, "I was ready to leave home."

"For me it was like crossing over the river," Martha said. "Fifteen was—ugh, I don't want to even think about it! Miserable all the time. Miserable in that stinky little village of Homers Mills where I lived. But I was made all over, brand new, on my sixteenth birthday. That was when I knew I was going to be an artist."

When I went up to my room later, I was still buzzed. I threw my presents down on the desk and stood in front of the mirror to see what I could see. I decided to sing a song. "And what do you think I saw? And what do you think I saw? The other side of the mountain, the other side of the mountain, the other side of the MOUNTAIN," I bellowed.

"Hey, what's going on up there," Gene called.

"I'm signing, I mean singing," I said, sticking my head out of the door. "I'm singing in my magnificent singing voice." I closed the door. "You are one hell of a singer," I told myself. "And you are also one hell of a young jackass." I snorted with jackassy cheer, *hee hee hee hee,* and fell back on my bed, thinking of the girl with the little gold birds pinned to her ears.

Seven

A couple of days later, I stood outside the Nut Shoppe, leaning against the window with my arms folded, trying for a casual I-just-happen-to-be-here effect. A warm wind rattled windows and blew papers down the street. From the corner of my eye I could see the girl behind the counter, waiting on a couple of kids. Any moment now, as soon as I had my opening remarks down pat, I was going to walk into the shop.

Hi! (Friendly.) *My name is Pete.* (Informative.) *What's your name?* (Nosy! Try again.)

I saw you working here. (Really observant.) *You must get sick of eating peanuts.* (Nooo kidding.) *Or maybe you prefer cashews?* (What is this, a survey on eating habits?)

Hello. (Good opening line.) *You're new on this job.* (Straightforward, anyway.) *I want to be your friend.* (Beautiful. Three sentences right out of Dick and Jane. From such a sensational beginning, no telling what mad, fantastic conversation would follow. *I am sixteen. How old are you? I am a sophomore in high school. What grade are you in?*

I pulled at the still-stiff collar of my new shirt. Usually I wouldn't wear a shirt this starched. A sacrifice for the Peanut Princess. My jeans were clean, too, and I'd replaced the missing shoelace in my sneakers. What more could mortal man do?

A woman wearing black trousers tight at the ankles and little strapped high-heeled red shoes passed me. Pretty sexy stuff for old Winston town. Maybe she'd turn back, put her hand on my arm. *Hello, there.* Wonderful voice, like Meryl Streep. *I like younger men.*

I crossed and uncrossed my arms, cleared my throat, peered down at my sneakers. Any moment now, I was going to do it. I was going to walk into the Nut Shoppe and say—something. But just in case the Princess happened to look out the window and notice me, I put on a thoughtful, curious expression. *Hi, do you like working downtown? It's my favorite place. Yours, too? What a coincidence!*

Would a princess be apt to like dirty old downtown? I toed a greasy hamburger paper. On the corner two men were working with jackhammers. A bus huffed past. Probably she hated working downtown. Should I start by telling her I lived downtown, only a few blocks away? Or would it be more urbane and sophisticated to put it down a little? *It's definitely scummy and noisy around here. On the other hand, it's also not boring. For a parochial little town like Winston, we get quite a mix of characters downtown. And where else can you find so much going on?*

If she said she hated downtown and loved suburbia, malls and all, would I still want to know her? (Yes.) I'd point out to her that convenient as malls were, they were also phony. Unnaturally clean. Cut off from the weather, with dead air and canned music. The world could come to an end and you'd never know it in a mall, for God's sake, I'd say. These places are inhuman, I'd tell her. She'd probably never thought about it that way before, and she'd

46

be so impressed with me that she'd want to know my name and . . .

And what? What then? If I actually did carry on an entire conversation with her, what was the next step? Ask her for a date? How? I had never done anything like that. I didn't think I could. No, I couldn't. How would I do it? Just say it? Say what? *I want a date with you?*

Maybe I should start off by asking her where she lived? Was that too personal? Suppose I told her how Gene and I lived right here, right in the middle of downtown. *That's fascinating!* she'd say, and then she'd want to know all about me. But I'd be modest. *Oh, there's not much to tell. No, no, I'd rather hear about you.*

A man in a camel's hair coat walked into the shop. I watched through the window. He was smiling at her, talking . . . He'd paid for his purchase, but he lingered, leaning on the counter. What was the matter with me? *Walk right in. Open your mouth and and talk. Come on, you coward!*

What happened then was I heard my father's voice. *Be proud, you're a Connors.* I looked around uneasily, as if the people on the street could hear it, too. And then my mother's voice chimed in. *We love you, darling, but there are so many children in the world* . . .

I twisted around, walked away. *If we could have done it any other way, you know we would have . . . Leaving you was the hardest part . . . But we know you understand and you'll be brave, that's your contribution to the struggle . . .*

When had they said that? The first time I saw them after I came to live with Gene? The second time? The third time? Eight years, three visits. Oddly, it was the first visit I remembered most vividly.

"Uncle" Marti, the same white-haired man who had brought me to Gene, showed up again and took me off on another trip. I think I was very frightened. Maybe he told me he was taking me to Laura and Hal, but if so I didn't believe him. I'd just about gotten my footing with Gene, and now they were taking me away again. I blanked out, slept for hours. When Marti woke me up, it was dusk and we were in the country, parked in front of a row of little cabins. A sign with a big arrow and a smile face said BRIGHT'S CLEAN MOTEL. TV. VACANCY.

I staggered after Marti toward one of the little cabins. He opened the door and stood aside for me to enter. Then he was gone and I was in a dark little room with two people I'd never seen before.

"Pax," the bearded man said, "it's Daddy." But Hal had never had a beard. And the fat, dark-haired woman said she was Laura. Laura, who was red-haired and slender and beautiful? I flattened myself against the door. I knew what it was—it was a trick to make me talk. The fat one pulled off her hair and was suddenly redhaired. She held out her arms. "Baby, baby." She was crying. I let myself be hugged. I would never tell them anything, even if they hit me with whips and clubs.

The people sat me down between them and asked me questions and kept hugging me and kissing me, and after a while I knew it was Laura and Hal. I started to cry and there was a knock on the door, Uncle Marti came in, and I was taken away again.

Now, at the corner by the big clock in front of Winston Savings Bank, I stopped. *Out, Laura and Hal, I don't want you here now. Out. Out.* A deep breath, think about the Peanut Princess, only her, nothing else. This isn't your Pax world. This is you, Pete Greenwood, and you want to know that girl. Go for it.

48

I turned and walked back to the Nut Shoppe, loose, not hurrying, resolute this time. Just a moment of hesitation, then I opened the door. The warm odor of roasting peanuts filled the little room. Today, her hair hung loose around her face and she wore a smock of some pale color. I stared at her, entranced. Then she spoke.

"May I help you?"

"Hi." My hand described a friendly arc in the air. She didn't respond. The aliens sometimes take awhile to warm up. "I want—uh—haven't made up my mind yet." I drifted down the counter, hands in my back pockets, staring at the bins of nuts with an intelligent expression. Almonds . . . walnuts . . . raw peanuts . . . Brazil nuts . . .

A woman with an armful of books entered. "A pound of those sugared walnuts, please."

The girl scooped walnuts into a white bag and weighed them. The woman paid, took her change, and left.

"Have you decided?" She wore several gold necklaces and the little gold bird earrings.

Hi! I know you don't know me, but I want to know you . . . Hi! This may sound weird since we don't know each other, but I can't stop thinking about you . . . Hi, there. My name is Pete. I thought we should get acquainted . . .

"Do you *want* something?" she said, looking at me suspiciously. Did she think I was a thief? DARING DAYLIGHT ROBBERY NETS SKINNY THIEF 200 POUNDS OF ROASTED PEANUTS. POLICE SET UP ROADBLOCKS.

"Peanuts," I said, as if inspired.

"How much?"

"What?"

"How—much?" she said distinctly, and then repeated in a loud voice, *"How much? One pound?"*

She obviously thought I was mentally deficient. I

49

tried to retrieve lost ground. "Fabulous!" She stared at me. "Right," I amended lamely.

She filled a bag, put it on the counter. I noticed that her nails were bitten to the quick. So, the Princess had at least one bad habit. I picked up the bag and started out.

"Hey!" she said. "You!"

I turned hopefully. That bellow wasn't exactly the sweet tones I'd been fantasizing about, but still, she was calling me. We were getting someplace.

"You didn't pay me."

I dug in my pocket, spilled change on the counter.

"I'd have to pay for that pound of peanuts out of my own pocket," she said. "It's people like you who make it hard for people like me."

"It was a mistake. I'm sorry, I didn't mean—"

"Oh, sure."

I gave up and went toward the door.

"Hey!"

I turned again. Maybe she ought to hire out as a football coach. She would never need a megaphone.

"You shorted me."

"What?"

"You *shorted* me." She held out her hand. "Not enough money."

Did she think I'd done it on purpose? Trusting soul. "How much?"

"Fifty-eight cents," she said, like a judge pronouncing sentence on a mass murderer.

You wanted to get to know this girl, Pax? Terrific. You are an astute judge of character. She could really brighten up your life.

I dug in my pockets and threw change down on the counter.

We glared at each other. I glared longer. Her eyes dropped first. Ha! Flushed with triumph, I wheeled and marched to the door.

"Hey!" she yelled for the third time. Big vocabulary, too.

"What now?"

"Your peanuts," she said, holding out the bag, and this time her eyes added, *Stupid.*

Eight

"Hi, Drew!" Wendy Varner, in a short pleated white skirt and a long red sweater, passed us in the hall, smiling, showing gorgeous teeth. "Hi, Pete," she added in a friendly way, but with a lot less enthusiasm.

I wondered if I should ask Drew's advice about the girl in the Nut Shoppe. Despite the—how to say it politely?—unfriendly note on which I had left the shop the week before, I was still thinking about the Peanut Princess. I kept playing over that scene in the shop and making it come out differently. In the new improved version, *she* was blushing, shy, sweet. *I* was manly, gruff, in control.

Hello! I'd like to get to know you and that's why I'm here. Are you interested?

From what I'd seen of the Peanut Princess, she would:

1. Annihilate me with a vicious stare.

2. Bark MYOB!

or

3. Call the fuzz and have me arrested for violating her privacy.

Choose one of the above. Then answer the following questions: Why had I fixed on her? Why did I continue to think about her? If I had to obsess, couldn't I obsess over someone sweet and pleasant? How about Hitler's sister?

In the chem lab, Sharon Karlin perched on the edge of my desk, the better to talk to Drew. "Did you see 'Three's Company' last night? It was a scream. It was humor!"

Why couldn't I obsess about Sharon? She certainly looked good enough with those spatters of freckles across her cheeks. Catching my eye, she smiled. She was wearing a white coverall with a polka-dotted handkerchief sticking out of the front pocket. I stared covertly at her breasts. Sharon and I were buddies. About once a week we did our math homework together in study hall. Once she'd called me at home to find out how to work a problem and then stayed on the phone for at least half an hour extra. I could have fallen in love with her in that half hour. The next day I'd wanted to rush up to her and say something terrific, at least give her the sort of bedroom-eyes look that Drew specializes in, the one that says everything without words. Instead, a desperate kind of shyness or fear had gripped me and I hadn't even talked to her for the rest of the week.

Today, by the time lunch rolled around, I had made up my mind to give the Peanut Princess another chance. After school I spent just long enough at a meeting of the History Club to keep Totie Golden, our faculty sponsor and my favorite teacher, from sinking into despair. Mrs. Golden was skinny, dark-haired and incredibly intense about history.

When we had our first club meeting back in September, she told us she wanted to inspire the same love of history in us that had been inspired in her by her high school history teacher, Kenneth Glad. She said his name as though he'd been a saint. "A rare and beautiful man! He taught history with compassion. He taught it with intelligence. With attention to the people who lived along the fringes of the great tides. Our books are full of explorations, war, and revolutions, but as my mentor, Kenneth Glad, often reminded us, never forget, never, never never forget that history is people."

That first meeting, when Mrs. Golden had asked us to call her Totie, there had been ten of us. Now there were only three left—me, Bambi Wiurka, and Robert Rizzo. We were a pretty tight little group, despite the fact that we all went our separate ways, not only outside History Club, but even inside it. We were all reading about different periods, different places. Every Monday we got together in Totie's classroom, and right away the talking and the yelling and the questions started. When our meeting most sounded like a street brawl, Totie just leaned back in her chair and let us go.

For me, the weekly meetings had come to be glad spots—no pun intended, although Kenneth Glad's name and presence were invoked so often by Totie that I thought I'd know the short, crew-cut history teacher in a roomful of strangers. Today, though, I really didn't have history on my mind. After half an hour I slouched out with a wave to Totie. No explanations needed.

Outside, the sky was big and blue. I had spent the first eight years of my life in a rather large, nearly skyless city that I thought was the entire world; then the next eight years here in Winston, living with a fair amount of sky, lots of trees, and one foot out the door: one foot waiting to be joined by the other foot in a fast getaway the moment Laura and Hal gave the word.

I jogged the couple of miles downtown, easy going

at first, all downhill. Past the worn granite Presbyterian church, a big bunch of little houses with neat neat lawns, past Leon's Barber Shop, and a wave to Leon, the lizardy barber with his black patent-leather hairpiece.

A car full of girls went by, their faces pasted to the windows. I kicked my heels up a little higher and zipped past the four corners with four gas stations, held my nose as I went by the pharmaceutical factory that hung a toilet smell over the whole area, and clattered over the bridge, below which rushed not water but gleaming streams of cars on the Interstate.

I had to slow down for the traffic light at Jefferson Boulevard. As I crossed, dodging cars, I memorized three license plates, just for the practice.

Now came the part when I didn't feel so lithe and athletic, running uphill. On the last stretch, I checked my time by the red digital clock on the Kappa Insurance Building, Winston's eight-story skyscraper. I was doing a nine-minute mile. Oh, well.

I'd left History Club early because of the so adorable Peanut Princess, but instead of going straight there, I played the coward and checked in at Greenwood's Optometry Center first. Delaying tactics.

"Your uncle's with a patient," Silky said. "Do you want to go to the post office for me?"

"Yes. No."

"Which one?"

"No, not now. Maybe later. I've got something to do. Tell Gene I'll be back in a little while."

The shop where the girl worked was only a short sprint from my uncle's office. I didn't run though, I didn't trot, I didn't even walk fast. I did cross Water Street against the light. Maybe I'd get hit by a car—then I wouldn't have to go through with this. Better still, she'd come out of the shop, see me lying bleeding on the street, and realize it was her heartless attitude that had ruined my life.

I stopped in Frank's Smokery and bought the new issue of *Time*. Once, sitting in a hamburger shop with Drew while he talked about baseball, I had idly opened *Newsweek* (I think it was *Newsweek*), and there, in the Update section, were little circled head shots of Hal and Laura. FEMMER LAB BOMBERS: WHERE ARE THEY NOW?

I must have gone into some kind of shock. My head heated up as if I'd been shoved into a pot of boiling water. I dropped the magazine onto the seat next to me. Drew was still talking, but I didn't hear a word. I had gone deaf. His mouth moved, he jumped up, swung an imaginary bat. I bent furtively over the magazine, staring at the pictures of my parents, my eyes fixed and blurring. The pictures weren't new to me; in fact, they were pictures I'd seen before in some newspaper article or other.

Yes, I knew these pictures, yet seeing them in a magazine I had just bought terrified me. What if Drew looked at those pictures and *knew?* Was it madness to think that way? Total paranoia? Why would Drew make a connection between Laura Glazer Connors and Hal Connors, the radical peace bombers, and his friend, Pete Greenwood?

Because you look like your mother. Because you're a strange duck. Because you act furtive, as if you have something to hide. Because you lie. Every day of your life, you live a lie. Because one of these days, people are going to know. And when they know—when they know what your parents did and who they are, when they know all that—what do you think they're going to think of you? They're going to shun you. Yes, you— you not-normal-person, you not-all-American-boy, you not-Pete. You're going to be a pariah. A leper. An

56

untouchable. They'll know who you are, what you are, you liar, you poseur, you pretender, you—.

I fought it. I fought the thoughts. No. Drew won't know. Nobody knows. Nobody has guessed. Why should Drew? Why should anybody? Yet I sat there and felt everything inside me go watery and bleak.

Now I stuck *Time* in my back pocket to read at home and did the my-mind-is-blank trick. I was good at that. A kind of concentration that forced everything out, as if my mind were a room I'd just emptied, blank and dark. I thought about walking, that was allowable, how the body knew to put one foot down and the other foot up, but if you thought about it, it would unsettle your whole rhythm. There were things you did you couldn't think about—just let your body take care of it.

By the time I got to the Nut Shoppe, I was back in the present, striding right along and promising myself that this time I would go straight in. No standing around working up my nerve stuff. I did it, too, walked in on the heels of an older couple.

"Give me some of those walnuts in the shell," the man said. "Last time they weren't so good. I don't think they were fresh. Are they fresh this time?"

"Yes," the girl said. "They're always fresh."

The man tugged at his jacket. "Well, they weren't fresh the last time." The woman stood to one side, her eyes on the ceiling. "Give me two pounds," the man said. "They'd better be fresh."

I threw the man a look. *Comes the revolution, you go first.* Besides the bird earrings, Princess was wearing gold chains today. Very royal. I wandered down to the short leg of the L-shaped counter, where I'd first seen her sitting and reading. Books were piled up next to a notebook. I craned my neck. Cary Longstreet. Her name and phone number were printed across the top of the notebook!

The bell on the door dinged. The couple left and the store was empty except for me.

"You want something?" she said.

"Hi. Remember me?" Great opening. *Sure, you're the idiot who forgot his peanuts.*

"No."

Good. Off to a fresh start. Still—was I that forgettable? "I was in here the other day. Last week."

"A lot of people come in here. Do you want to buy something?" Her broad, high, shining forehead looked disdainful and cool. Definitely the forehead of a princess of the royal line. *Your Grace, granted, I'm not royalty of your breed. All the same, democracy is the watchword these days. Can you find it in your heart to give a mere commoner a few of your precious moments?* I slouched, elbow on the counter to proclaim my poise, and noticed that she wore too much makeup. Her eyes were covered with goop. Still, with her hair drawn back with a red ribbon, she looked cute as hell.

I jingled my change fervently. "To tell the truth, I still haven't eaten all the peanuts I bought the other day." What a splendid nugget of useless information. Was there anyting else silly or pointless I could say? "I don't even like peanuts that much," I blundered on.

She yawned, her hand with the bitten nails delicately patting her opened mouth.

I was boring her! Why not? I was boring myself. "Look," I said, gripping the counter, "I—I—" Her brown eyes, steady and wary, disconcerted me. "I have a friend who thinks you're beautiful. He wants to know you. He wants to be your friend. His name is Drew." I heard these words coming out of my mouth with total disbelief. Drew? I had to bring Drew into this?

Suddenly her cheeks flushed, her eyes opened

wide, her whole face changed—it was the strangest thing. One minute I was looking at Cool Princess Yawnski and the next I was looking at a little kid, just a real little kid with huge eyes that said, *Don't play with my feelings, don't tell me things that aren't true, don't hurt me that way.*

Again I had that same sense of urgency I'd had when I first saw her—that she was different, special, someone I had to know.

Then—it almost seemed by an effort of will—she became the Princess again. It was like a window closing. "What do you want?" she said.

I want to know you. I want to know who you really are and why I keep thinking that you're different from other girls, different in a way I don't understand. "I want—ah, my name is Pete," I said. "Pete Greenwood. And you're—"

She cut me off. "I thought your name was Drew."

"That's my friend."

"Oh, yes! Your friend."

"I really do have a friend Drew."

"Do you?" She looked me in the eye.

"Yes."

"And he wants to know me?"

"No," I said. "That part wasn't true. It's me."

There we were, looking straight at each other, and I was finally telling the truth and saying what I'd meant to say, and she was smiling. Yes! She smiled at me. Then the bell sounded and the man with the walnuts came storming back in. "These nuts are stale. Who's the manager here? I want his name. I want to tell him a thing or two." His wife stood off to one side looking up at the ceiling again. Then a bunch of kids came in, then a whole rush of people, and after a while I left.

Nine

I sloshed a rag around the sink (my turn to do the dishes), thinking about the girl with the gold birds in her ears. It drove me crazy, but in a pleasant way. *Cary Longstreet.* Her name. Her phone number. I hadn't tried to remember, the information had just stuck in my head. It was the same way with license plates. They stuck in my mind whether I wanted them there or not. Some nights when I had trouble falling asleep, license plates did a sheep-jumping-over-fence number in my mind. And there'd been plenty of mornings when I'd come awake mumbling a plate number I'd seen days before.

The house was quiet, too quiet. Gene was at the theater, auditioning for a part in a new production. The floors creaked, and every once in a while a squirrel ran across the roof, sounding like a whole cavalry corps. You didn't think there was wildlife downtown? Think again. Not just squirrels and chipmunks and hordes of pigeons, starlings, and English sparrows, but raccoons and skunks, both of which have visited us. Once we even had a red fox streak through our backyard.

The phone rang. "Hello!" I should have given Cary my phone number. *Call me anytime.* "Is Jenny there?" a woman asked. "What number do you

want?" "Oh, sorry, I must have the wrong number."
I hung up and waited. Wrong numbers always call
twice. Sure enough, the phone rang again. "Is Jenny
there? . . . Oh, sorry!"

After that, silence. Too much silence. When I'm
alone in the house, which is fairly often, weird things
sometimes happen in my head. I'm not scared, not in
the sense of a little kid thinking the bogeyman is
coming. But if I don't watch it, don't keep myself
busy, I start working over stuff in my mind. Stuff.
This and that, and here and now, and yes and no, and
how come and why not and what if. Stuff. Stuff about
my parents.

Tonight I'd been doing okay, lots of positive
thoughts about Princess Cary, until the phone call
broke the spell. I began to wonder if it had been an
actual wrong number—or a message from Laura and
Hal, a coded message that I had to unscramble.

That thought was like a bomb going off in my
mind. After it came the fallout. It started with a
single question, an old question, a familiar question.
Where are Laura and Hal right now? What are they
doing? Are they still out there somewhere? They've
always managed to get letters out to me before . . .

So what? What do you know? Everything changes,
the world can change in a moment, isn't that the
point of their work, we're three minutes from dooms-
day, they're crying out for people to wake up and
take notice . . . Yes, it could be happening now, nuclear missiles flying over the ocean . . . Now you're
standing here slurping ice cream out of the carton,
and in another moment you could be nothing but a
heap of radioactive ashes . . . And not just that, little
things, everyday things, change too, you ought to
know that better than anyone else . . . Don't take
anything for granted, ever . . . Today Drew is your
friend, tomorrow he . . . No. Not Drew. He's steady,

61

solid . . . Are you sure? Yes. Really? Yes! So you don't think he ever has second thoughts about you? You don't think he and Deirdre ever talk about you?

That Pete, there's something bloody weird about him, something not quite—right?

Oh, Pete's all right, a real character . . .

I don't know, Drew, it's not just that he's a character, did you ever think Pete has some kind of secret? Something he keeps from you? How come he never wants to talk about his parents?

Nuttiness. Craziness. Paranoia Pete. Nobody was talking about me. Were they? How did I know? How did I know anything? How did I know Laura and Hal were still alive? Two months since I'd had a letter . . . Maybe they'd been found . . . were being held prisoner . . . questioned, maybe even tortured. Held without trial? *Tortured?* In this country? You are weird. This is America . . . So ? Bad things never happen here? It could happen, it could definitely happen . . .

A private organization . . . a vigilante group . . . What about those kids who were kidnapped and deprogrammed . . . held against their will? Anything can happen. Anytime. It was possible the last letters were fakes, forgeries, and . . . No, no, no, no, no.

Questions, answers, possibilities, comments, lectures, fantasies. On and on my mind raced. And in between all the mind-fire, I paced the rooms, glanced out each window, peered into the shadows, looking for *them,* the agents, the FBI, the ones who were looking for my parents. Are *they* out there? Are *they* watching the house?

When I lived with my parents, we knew *they* were always somewhere out there. They showed up at rallies, good-looking men in pressed suits, hanging back in the crowd, taking photos. *They* parked their cars and took notes and pictures when Laura and Hal passed out leaflets in shopping centers or in front of factories, and often *they* were simply there, parked across the street from the building where we lived.

We were on the third floor. I slept on a cot in the hall. We hadn't much money—Laura and Hal were always losing their jobs, even though they were brilliant (I heard their friends say it), because they were so committed to their work for a better world, for peace on earth, the dream of Christ, who, Laura told me, was born a Jew like her; because that dream came before anything else. And when we climbed the dark little staircase to our apartment, we sang songs, sometimes just weary, end-of-the-day nonsense. Laura had a wonderful husky voice. It sent shivers through me. "And up we go and up we go and up we go," she sang, "and boodle bo, boodle bo, boodeley doodeley boodle bo, just two more flights to go!"

And she'd wait for me to take out my key and unlock the door. And then later if we had to go out to buy a quart of milk because Hal had forgotten, and Laura too, and the sweet boy (that was me) needed his milk, *they'd* be there in their car, and my mother would see them and wave. *They* scared me, but not her, and not my father. "Oh, *them,*" Hal would say, "*they* have to make a living too, don't they? But isn't it too bad, son, that they have to do it by following people like us who are only trying to make the world a better place? What a crime we're committing," he'd roar, laughing, and sweep me into his arms and hug me.

I looked out the window again. The street was empty. Empty. Empty. Dark and still, and the phone was still, and the house was still, and to stop my mind I had to do something sane and ordinary.

Phone Drew, eat a pot of spaghetti, make fudge, read a book. Get back to basic strategy for avoiding paranoia when alone: Keep busy. Constructively busy. Which meant no more *stuff*. No more obsessing. And no sly, nutty pranks, like calculating down to the hour and the minute how long it had been since I'd seen Laura and Hal. But except for my foray into the Royal Peanut Kingdom, I hadn't been feeling healthily constructive since my birthday.

A week of being low, itchy, antsy, a week of finding it hard to stop spinning, to sit still anywhere, anytime. Because when I did slow down, I sensed a kind of plummeting low in my gut, as if something were just about to go wrong. Only that morning I'd awakened sweating, dripping—not the good old, bad old White Terror, but close, close.

I told myself now to get moving in the right direction, turn off the mind, listen to music, do something normal and good for me. Instead, I went upstairs to my room, straight to the fat manila envelope hidden under my mattress. An absurd place to hide anything! Wouldn't it be the first place *they'd* look? If *they* ever found me, they'd tear up this room. No, I had to move that envelope, but where? Weren't my other hiding places just as absurd? The back of my closet behind the tennis racket and the box of outgrown clothes and toys. The space between the bottom drawer and the bottom of my bureau. And what about the old stone cistern in the cellar? That had nearly been a disaster because of the damp. I'd lost a few of the letters, dried out the rest (there were still smudgy illegible parts), and spent numerous Saturdays in the library making fresh copies of all the articles and stories. Of course, if *they* came *they* wouldn't care about the library stuff. That was public record. It was the letters they'd scrutinize. Yet, although for one year I'd burned my parents' letters, I couldn't bring myself to do that again.

I emptied the manila envelope onto my desk, sorting and arranging the letters and articles. Phrases jumped out at me. ". . . picked up four people for questioning in connection with the bombing of Femmer Lab," "allegedly members of the organization known as Air, Water, Earth," "who saw a woman enter the lab about noon said," "This is the most difficult letter we have ever had to write," "couple and son being sought," "Jameson and Kin Udall, a graduate student who had been working with Dr. Jameson, were buried today," "My dear son, your mother and I," "getting off the elevator and saw the woman drop the package into a wastebasket," "If there had been any other way than leaving you behind," . . .

My parents had been newspaper copy for a lot longer than they'd been in hiding. Actually, the oldest newspaper story about them was nearly as old as I was.

It was a human interest story that had appeared when Laura and Hal were attending college in Connecticut. YOUNG COUPLE WITH CHILD ATTEND COLLEGE TOGETHER, SHARE EVERYTHING. Then a picture of them, side by side, in their married-student housing. Laura, slender, beautiful, serious, a thin freckled face, pushing her hair behind her ears; Hal, shorter, wider, his eyebrows a thick slash across his forehead, grinning straight at the camera, that wide grin I remembered above all else about him; and both of them barefoot in the little dark room. I was there, too, standing up in a playpen. " 'How do you manage to keep house, take care of a child, and study for your classes?' 'Not easy,' the freckled redhead chuckled. 'Does Hal help with the housework?' 'He'd better,' the pert mother and student giggled."

In the next article, no giggling, no chuckling. A

picture of my parents in their graduation robes, Laura again with that I'm-looking-straight-into-your-eyes seriousness, and Hal hoisting me up to his shoulders, his mortarboard cocked over my eyes. GRADUATES PROTEST COMMENCEMENT SPEAKER. " 'We have become numb to the poisoning of our environment and the madness of nuclear war overshadowing our lives,' honors graduate Laura Glazer Connors said today after she and several dozen other graduates, including her husband, Hal Connors, staged a walkout to protest General William H. Adderson's appearance at their commencement. 'The human race is in danger of destroying itself. Do we need more weapons? More generals? More nuclear bombs? When I look at my son, I find that I can no longer live with myself if I ignore these realities.' With the Connors couple in the picture above is their three-year-old son, Pax."

Without the Connors couple in the room before you is their sixteen-year-old son, Pete. All at once I knocked everything to the floor, letters, articles, and pictures. I ran down the back stairs into the kitchen and stood in front of the open refrigerator, stuffing in hunks of cold barbecued chicken.

The phone rang. "Shut up!" It rang again. I yanked the receiver off its cradle. "Hello!"

"Pete?" Martha said.

"Oh. Hi, Martha."

"You okay?"

"Oh—sure—"

"Is Gene around?"

"He's at the theater for the auditions."

"The auditions? Darn! I was going to show up and it totally slipped my mind. So he's out? Phooey! I'm feeling sort of down in the dumps. I was hoping Gene could talk me out of it."

I sat down on the floor. "That makes two of us."

"You're blue?" she said, as if my being depressed was one of the seven wonders of the world. "What have you got to be blue about?"

"Sixteen is the best time of life, right, Martha?"

"Yes, it is."

"Think again."

"Maybe you don't know it now, but basically you've got it made. Let me tell you how things look from the outside. Give you a little perspective, Pete. To begin with, your uncle Gene's a real special person. The two of you live in a great house—do you know how many people would give their eyeteeth to live in a house like yours? You've got no worries about school, you're a smart guy, you'll go to college for sure, you don't have money worries, you're cute, too. So, what's the beef? Okay, your parents are dead. Sure, that's not easy, I would never suggest it is, but you have to admit it's years behind you and you've gone through it all, you've adjusted, am I right?"

"Right."

"So what's got you down?"

"What's got *you* down, Martha? As far as I can see, you've got it made. You're an artist, you're independent, you are doing what you love. Also, you're cute. Okay, I know you don't make much money, I don't want to sound like not being able to pay your bills is Little League, but you've gone through it for years and you're well-adjusted about it, am I right?"

"Pete—!"

"What's the matter, Martha, you can give it, but you can't take it?"

"You can be a definite pain in the ass."

"I thought I was your ideal teenage boy. You said that last week."

"I never."

"Your very words."

"I take it all back."

"You said you really adored me and that I was sweet."

"I must have been stoned."

"Excuses, excuses." I walked into the dining room, pulling the long red phone cord after me.

"You know what I did today, Pete— Do you have homework to do? Am I keeping you from something?"

I thought of the letters and clippings all over my floor. "I'd rather talk to you."

"Today a man with a face exactly like a white potato asked me to do his portrait. I hated doing it, Pete! It wasn't even a warty, interesting potato face. It was just one of those blah faces. I know that's unfair. It's not his fault his face is totally without merit—but all I could think was, Damn! I'm never going to be any good as an artist. I'm going to spend the rest of my life in this crummy little corner painting potato faces, and I'll never be Eakins or Sargent or Rosa Bonheur or anyone."

"I guess not."

"Thanks."

"I was just agreeing with you, Martha."

"Learn a little tact, sweetie! It'll go a long way in your relations with women."

"What relations?"

"Oooh, is that it? Well, look, Pete, it's going to happen. I know you think I'm doing a number on you when I tell you these are your best years, but I'm not that insensitive. I know it can be hard sometimes in the teens, but I'm here to tell you it does not get easier as you get older. In some ways, yes, things are better, you get some stuff sorted out. But in other ways, look—avenues get closed off. I'm thirty and here I am—I don't know if you can really understand what I'm saying. There's such a huge difference in our ages. Fifteen years. That's a whole lifetime."

"Fourteen years. And I'm not that young. And you're not that old."

"Hey! You just learned tact. Also, you've just made my favorite teenage boy list again."

Later, upstairs in my room, I got everything back into the manila envelope and put it under the mattress. Out of sight, out of mind. A fine old cliché that didn't work. I pulled the envelope out again and shook out one of the letters from my mother.

Years ago when I received this letter, I had carried it around with me and read it over and over. I knew it nearly by heart. Now I read part of it, then I just didn't want to go on with it. I put my head on the desk. Maybe I fell asleep . . . The house floated around me, cut off from the warm breathing world, a box in dark space and I, a frozen pebble, rattling at its center.

My dear, dear son,

I think about you constantly, with longing and joy. I dream about you often. Just last night I had a wonderful dream! You were small in it, maybe four or five years old, and standing on a hill waving to me. "Laura," you called. "Laura, hurry up, I want chocolate-chip-cookies, a whole bag of them!" (Your favorite cookies!) And in the dream you laughed and reached out your hands to me with so much love that my heart seemed to melt. I ran toward you. Then I woke up, as happy as if we'd had a real visit!

How are you, how are you, how are you? I mean that in every sense of the word. I'm sure your health is good, you never were sick a day, but you haven't forgotten (or let Uncle forget), have you, that you ought to have your teeth checked every six months? (Unfortunately, you got my teeth and not your father's.) Are you helping with the housework? Are you reading anything interesting? Are you studying hard in school and doing good work? I say good, but I'm sure it's excellent! If school is not enough of a challenge for you, *make* it a challenge. Don't ever lean back, in school or anywhere else, with a "ho-hum" attitude.

It's now been almost two years that we've been separated. Sometimes I get so terribly sad thinking about all the days and weeks, all the months that I haven't spent with you, all the special moments we've lost. I won't lie to you, a great sadness lies on my heart and that is missing you. Every day I miss you, every day I think about you and wish I could see you even for five minutes."

It's not yet meant to be, but soon, I hope, very soon. Until then, my dearest boy, I send you all the love in my heart.

Mom

Ten

Late Saturday afternoon, I put in a few hours in Gene's office, cleaning and washing windows. It was raining when I left, and as I closed the door, a black car that had been parked across the street pulled away into traffic. There were two men in the car, both wearing fedoras. Fedoras? In Winston? I turned abruptly and walked the other way. Was it *them?* Had they found me? Had they been watching the office all day? Would they be waiting in front of the house for me?

The rain came down hard as bullets. People scurried for shelter, holding newspapers and pocketbooks over their heads. At the corner, near the bus stop, I saw Cary Longstreet. She was standing in a cluster of people sheltering under the plexiglass dome. Her arms were full of packages. I should have said something. *Hello. Hi. Hey, there.* She had smiled at me the last time I saw her. I should have spoken, but instead I wheeled around again and ran back to our house, all thoughts of the two sinister men in fedoras forgotten.

A marvelous, foolproof plan had sprung full-blown into my mind. Go home, get Gene's umbrella, on the double back to the bus stop, slow down and walk casually by Cary. Then "see" her. *Now* talk. *Oh, hi!*

What a coincidence. Aren't you the girl from the Nut Shoppe? The bus hasn't come yet? Let me walk you home under my umbrella. I'd lift the umbrella over her head. I'd offer to carry her packages. Once we were on our way, the sun would come out. We'd talk. She'd admit that she had hardly thought of anything but me the whole week.

Great plan. Minor flaw. No umbrella. In the house I rampaged through the closets and cupboards, flinging things out, before I remembered seeing the umbrella standing open to dry in a corner of Gene's office.

I went out again. It was raining harder than ever. At the bus stop, there were four people huddled under the shelter—two little girls swinging ballet shoes and a couple, both in pea green sweatshirts, kissing.

I hung around for a while, I don't know why, just on the off-chance that Cary Longstreet had remembered some last-minute shopping and would appear again. Finally, thoroughly wet, I went back home.

Gene had been in and out. There was a note on the bulletin board. "Gone to the theater for audition results. Keep fingers and toes crossed. Ravioli in the fridge. Heat bread, make salad." I kicked off my sneakers and squished around the kitchen, heating up the ravioli and bread. I could call her. And say what? *I'm the guy who came into the Nut Shoppe last week and wanted to get to know you.* What if she had forgotten already that she'd smiled at me? What if she hung up on me? What if she yawned? What if she said, *Which guy who wanted to know me? Last week there were six, the week before, ten.*

I tortured myself for hours before I got up the

nerve to dial her number. A woman answered on the first ring. "Yancey residence."

"Hello?" I said.

"Yancey residence."

"Sorry, I must have the wrong number."

"Who do you want?"

"Cary? Cary Longstreet?"

"Who is this?"

"Uh—a friend—"

"Do you realize it's nearly ten o'clock at night? Don't you think that's a bit late to be calling Cary?"

"She's there?" I said. "She lives there?"

"Are you calling for Cary?"

"Yes."

"Well, she can't come to the phone right now. We can't have phone calls coming in this late. You call her tomorrow, but earlier."

I hung up and stood there, looking at the phone. Yancey residence? Then I heard Gene in the front hall. "Pete?" He came in, smiling broadly. "You see before you, sir," he said, his voice taking on an English accent, "Brassett!"

"Who?"

"Brassett, a college scout, otherwise known as a gentleman's gentleman. Shall I take the tray away now, sir? . . . Certainly, sir, anything you say, sir." He did a little heel-clicking number.

"You got the part you wanted."

"I did indeed. I tried out for Brassett and I got it. And one other little plum—I'm the understudy for Lord Fancourt Babberley who, as you no doubt don't know, plays the fake Charley's aunt."

"Oh."

" 'Oh, that is fine news, Uncle Gene. Congratulations, Uncle Gene. I'm really glad you got the part in *Charley's Aunt* that you wanted. And I think it's wonderful news, too, that you're understudying Lord Fancourt Babberley.' 'Well, thank you, Pete, I knew you'd be as enthusaistic as I am.' "

I looked at the phone again. "That's great, Uncle G, that's really great."

Eleven

The letter from my parents came at last. Two letters, actually. They were there on the front hall floor in front of the mail slot when I came home from school. They arrived in a single plain white envelope. This time it had been mailed from Little Rock, Arkansas. They had undoubtedly written the letters somewhere else and passed them on to someone they trusted, to pass on to someone else, to pass on to still another someone to mail. Maybe the chain was five people long, maybe it was ten people long. None of them had to be members of Air, Water, Earth, just sympathetic supporters. None of them would live in Little Rock. None of them would know any more than the person behind and the person ahead in the chain.

I held the envelope up to the light. An ordinary envelope of the kind that came in a box of one hundred. I turned it over several times, studying my neatly typewritten name. And I imagined Hal, with his blazing grin, or Laura, red hair tucked into a kerchief, going into a typewriter store. Maybe she would be wearing a wig, the way she had that time, years ago, when that man who called himself Uncle Marti had taken me to see her for an afternoon.

In the typewriter store, Laura would check out

various typewriters. She'd put the envelope into one of them and type my name and address. Then she'd shake her head regretfully. No, this typewriter was not exactly what she was looking for. And she'd stuff the envelope, as if without thought, into her pocket, and walk out.

I tore the envelope into bits, burned the pieces in the bathroom sink, and flushed away the ashes. For eight years, two or three times a year, I had done the same thing. Except the year I was twelve. That year, when I burned the envelopes, I also burned the letters, burned them unread. Didn't they always say the same thing? "My dearest son . . . We miss you . . . Your job is to go to school, learn and grow . . . Someday you will understand . . . Someday you will fully realize why we . . . We love you, but . . ."

That year I hated everything, my uncle, school, most of all my parents. I drew up lists of accusations against them, starting with *You left me,* going on from there, but always coming back to *You left me.*

Why did you set that bomb? Didn't you know what was going to happen? How could you be sure no one was in the lab? Why didn't you think about that? You left me. You don't love me. You love your stupid politics. You left me.

My voice was changing and so was I. I cut my heroes, Laura and Hal, down to size. They were dumb and stupid, they were selfish and crappy, and if they ever came back, they'd be sorry for the rest of their lives because I wouldn't ever go to live with them again. I imagined the scene, I saw Laura crying and Hal pleading. *Son, son, at least talk to us.* But I wouldn't say a word, I'd walk out on them and I wouldn't come back until they were gone.

Every day I wore the baseball cap Drew had given me and every night I repeated, *I'm Pete. I'm Pete. I'm*

Pete Greenwood. Pete Greenwood, school-skipper, baseball fan, a regular kid. Pete-not-Pax.

One warm spring evening I was out with Drew and some other boys. We passed our old elementary school and began throwing stones at the building. "Watch this one, you guys!" Direct hit. A spiderweb of cracks spread across a window. "Run!" someone yelled. "Come on, Pete, come on!"

They ran, but I walked. I strolled jauntily, as if nothing could ever bother me. In reality, I was in a state of shock, my heart shaking in my chest as I waited for the patrol car to pull up beside me and the police to spring out. *You're under arrest!* Me first. Then my parents. The logic was inescapable. My arrest would lead directly to theirs. I saw them being led into court in manacles, I saw their sad, reproachful eyes and the judge leaning down. *I sentence you both to life imprisonment . . .*

When I got home I was in a sweat and couldn't eat. I went out again. It was dusk, the stores were closing. I walked past the city parking lot, the bank, the newspaper building, walked as fast and purposefully as if I were looking for something. Yet I didn't know what it was or where I was going until I found it.

Behind the post office, which bordered on the Interstate, I climbed over a railing and half-slid down a muddy bank into a patch of scrubby woods. As soon as I stepped in, I knew this was why I'd left the house—to find this wedge of trees, this place out of time. Faint paths crisscrossed it like pencil markings. Birds and squirrels racketed. I stood under an enormous beech tree on the roots that spread out like gray crippled fingers over the ground and looked up through the canopy into the sky. The Interstate laced over, above, and around the woods, the world woven over me, but unable to reach me. The hum of traffic filtered through the trees. I lay down on the ground, clutching at the beech roots, and cried and swore to Laura and Hal that I didn't hate them, I didn't, I didn't . . .

After that day I started reading their letters again, reading them and saving them, but it was never quite the same as it had been before. Because now, always, somewhere in the far, back reaches of my mind, the other thoughts, the questions and accusations, were always there, always waiting. I didn't want them. I pushed them away, I resisted. Sometimes I was successful. Other times not. More and more I was unsuccessful—the questions came and I sensed something in me demanding that I face those questions, demanding that I answer them for myself. *Why did you leave me? Why did you set that bomb? What made you turn from demonstrations to bombs? Didn't you know what might happen? How could you be sure no one was in the lab? You thought about so much—why didn't you think about that?*

Now, after all the energy I'd put into being mad at my parents for not writing, I didn't read their letters right away. I threw them into my desk drawer and went out, not going anywhere, just walking and trying not to think. A boy in a red and black checkered shirt, plugged into an enormous silver radio slung over his shoulder, boogied past me. Buses rumbled down the street and the smell of exhaust fumes linked with the smell of fried food. Downtown smells. I liked being downtown, moving through the crowds, nobody looking at me, nobody noticing me. A safe feeling. I walked for a long time, went past the Nut Shoppe, but kept going. Today wasn't the day to go in there.

I didn't read the letters when I got home either. Gene and I ate supper and he went out, and I went upstairs to do homework. In the middle of studying theorems, I slammed the book shut. I couldn't concentrate and I wouldn't be able to until I read my parents' letters.

I read my father's letter first.

Dear Pax,

Another year has passed. You're sixteen now, nearly a man. I know custom says manhood doesn't come until your twenty-first birthday, but in your case, I cannot believe this. You've been through things that an ordinary boy hasn't. I know it's made a difference—matured you, made you wiser, grown you up faster. You have experienced, endured, survived—as have I. Life is a struggle, but we are armed for it. We are strong and become stronger while the forces opposing us must grow weaker with time because they are against the tide of history.

I haven't been able to be an ordinary father to you, but I think of you and about you the way any father does. I want you to believe this. Life has separated us, but we are still father and son. These have not been easy years for any of us, but we will come out stronger for them. Of that I am convinced. Now, on your birthday, I raise a cup to you, my son. Salud!

All my love,
Hal

And beneath his signature, with a little flourish, the word *Dad.*

I read his letter several times. The house was quiet, the windows closed, outside sounds muffled. After a while, I unfolded my mother's letter.

Dearest boy,

Happy birthday, dear one. This year I want to send you a poem that has often comforted me, in the hope that it will mean something very special to you, too. It is from the book *The Prophet* by the Syrian poet Kahlil Gibran.

Your children are not your children.

They are the sons and daughters of Life's longing for itself.

They come through you but not from you,
And though they are with you yet they belong not to you.
You may give them your love but not your thoughts,
For they have their own thoughts.
You may house their bodies but not their souls,
For their souls dwell in the house of tomorrow, which you cannot visit, not even in your dreams.

Do you understand what I'm saying? I am now and always will be your mother and I love you as I love my life, but you are not mine, you do not belong to me, you are your own person. We are separated, it's been many years, too many years, and yet this poem comforts me, tells me that although I haven't been able to be an everyday mother to you, we will both come through these times, these trials, with our love and respect for each other intact. Happy birthday, my darling. I send you more love than you can imagine. May we be reunited soon.

Your mother,
Laura

Later, in the shower, a memory, like a dream, came back to me . . . showering with my father, he was shampooing my hair, my head came just to his belly button . . . and outside the bathroom, my mother, laughing, calling, *Are you two going to be in there forever?*

Sixteen? A man? My own person? Clinging to the slick wet tile I was a child again, a little boy, shivering and close to tears.

Twelve

Every Wednesday and Friday, a big silver refrigerator truck out of Boston delivers fresh fish to Lombardi's Fish Market on Railroad Ave on the corner beneath the Interstate overpass. Gene gets ecstatic over eating fresh fish and if he can't get away from the office himself, he sends me over to Lombardi's.

Inside, a sign posted on the wall above the scale says, LOMBARDI'S FAMOUS FRESH FISH MARKET! WE HAVE SERVED THE PUBLIC FOR 50 YEARS NO ONE DOES IT BETTER THAN WE DO!!! I never read that sign without wondering what it is they do better than anyone else. I took my number card off the sprocket on the counter. The room is small and fishy smelling, and people were packed in like sardines (ha ha). Friday is actually the worst day to go to Lombardi's because, besides the fresh fish, they also sell fish and chips dinners. Hordes of people come just for that. The door opened and shut constantly as people poured in. All of a sudden I saw Cary Longstreet—or was it Yancey?—right in front of me. I hadn't even seen her come in, and now she was close enough to touch—but I wouldn't dare. She had that cool princess-of-the-realm look spread over her face like a mask. I had to remind myself of that little smile she'd given me, a fresh mischievous little smile that had given me heart.

"Cary—"I said, but just then the clerk called my number. "Twenty-four! Step up, please, don't hold other people up!" She wore a bloodstained white coat like a doctor.

I ordered two dozen clams and a pound of red snapper. "Clean it and leave the head on." Gene made a fish soup from the head. I glanced over my shoulder at Cary, wondering if she recognized me. She had moved away, toward the other end of the counter, where they sold the fish and chips.

Outside, I hung around, waiting for her. Practice being Drew, I told myself, give her that old Gregoretti smile, that old Gregoretti charm. As soon as she came out, I tossed her a big smile and said, "Hi!"

"Hi." She put the white bag of fish and chips into the saddlebag of a red boy's bike and rode off. Was that it? For one moment I looked after her in despair, then I ran after her. I caught up with her at the corner, where she was waiting for a break in the traffic.

"Hi," I said again. "Do you remember me at all? I'm Pete. I came into the shop—"

"I know. Yo're the one with the friend."

"No, I told you—the friend—forget him. I'm the one, I'm the guy who wants to know you."

"Mmm," she said, and pushed off.

I caught up with her again at the next corner. "Going the same way you are," I lied.

"Uh huh."

I ran after her, block after block, barely keeping her in sight. Once, twice, she glanced back at me. At the corner of Elm and Bridge streets, I had a lucky break when a policeman halted traffic for a funeral procession.

I trotted up to Cary. "Listen, don't you think I've

run far enough? How about giving me a ride? I'll pedal."

"You're nervy, aren't you?"

"Hey, I'm not fussy. I'll ride the handlebars."

"Where are you going?"

"Where are *you* going?"

"Home."

"What street?"

"Franklin Avenue."

"What do you know! Just where I'm going!"

"You live on Franklin?"

"I know someone who lives there." That was the truth—now.

"Who's that?"

Then another lucky break—I didn't have to answer. The policeman blew his whistle, beckoning the line of waiting cars forward, and Cary bumped off the curb.

"How about that ride?"

"You are a pest," she said, but she smiled.

"Don't you think it's a sign of character to be persistent? What's the verdict? Do I keep running or do I go to Franklin Avenue in style?"

She touched one of the little gold bird earrings. "Oh . . . why not? But I pedal."

I put my fish into the saddlebag next to her package and hopped up on the handlebars. She bent forward, her head almost touching my back. "This is great," I said.

"For you."

"Told you I'd be glad to—"

"No thanks. I don't let other people ride my bike."

"Afraid I'll steal it?"

"You can walk, you know."

"I'm not complaining. I saw you at the bus stop the other day when it was raining."

"I didn't see you." She bumped up the curb and

stopped in front of a little, brown-shingled house with a sagging porch and a tiny front yard. "All off. This is where I live."

I was surprised. Not a very impressive house for a princess.

"You'll have to walk the rest of the way to your friend's," she said.

"I have a confession to make." I held on to the handlebars. "My friend on this street is you."

"Nooo kidding."

I flushed. "I just wanted to get to know you."

"You are persistent, aren't you?"

"A persistent pest, I guess." I looked at her, hoping she'd deny I was pest. "Well, anyway, thanks for the ride. Now I have a long walk home."

"You don't even live around here?"

"I live downtown."

"Nobody lives downtown."

"Lots of people live downtown, not just us. Street people—"

"That's just fancy talk for bums."

I didn't want to get into an argument with her on the first day. "People live in the Y's, too," I said. "And there's the Jefferson Hotel—that's mostly older women—"

"Is that where you live, in the Y?"

"No, I live in a house. I'll show it to you sometime." A face appeared at a window. A girl with bangs and glasses tapped on the pane and beckoned to Cary. "Your sister's calling you," I said.

Cary wheeled the bike up onto the porch. " 'Bye, Pete, it was fun. Oh, wait! Your fish." She tossed me the package. I caught it and saluted her as she went inside.

Thirteen

"Yancey residence."

"Can I speak to Cary, please?"

"This is Cary."

"Hi! This is Pete."

"Who?"

"Pete. Pete Greenwood. The one you gave a ride on your bike. The fish market? Don't you remember me?"

"Of course I remember you."

"Well . . . hi, again! Ah . . . how're you doing?"

"Fine."

"Ah . . . just thought I'd call and say hello."

"Okay."

"So! . . . Hello.

"Hello."

"So, ah . . . Cary! It's great talking to you. Listen, didn't you just say 'Yancey residence'? Isn't your last name Longstreet?"

"What'd you say your last name was?"

"Greenwood. Green. Wood. Forest, trees, that's the way you remember it."

"All right, Pete Green Wood. How'd you get my phone number? I didn't give it to you."

"Ah . . ."

"And something else—how do you know my last name?"

"Would you believe I'm psychic?"

"No."

"How about—it came to me in a dream."

"You're a clown, aren't you?"

"Actually, I'm a very serious fellow."

"You don't sound it. Are you buzzed?"

"Not tonight. I'm giddy, Cary. Can you guess why?"

"Do you drink a lot?"

"Just a little wine sometimes. Why?"

"I don't like what drinking does to people. It makes them sloppy and disgusting. I used to drink some when I was younger, but no more."

"Sometimes it's nice to get away from yourself, to let go."

"Maybe. I still want to know how you got my phone number."

"Did you never hear of the great Sherlock Holmes who could re-create entire personalities from the merest details? What if I told you that I am Holmes reincarnated and that by riding the handlebars of your bike, I deduced your name and your phone number?"

"Look, can I have a straight answer?"

"You sound mad."

"I never get mad."

"Tell me your secret! I get mad all the time, I just suddenly—pow, I explode. But I'm not violent, don't worry; all I do is yell and stomp around and then I'm okay."

"You still haven't answered my questions."

"Okay, this is straight. I saw it on your notebook—"

"You snooped."

"Cary, I just happened to see it. Your notebook

was out on the counter—I didn't try to memorize your phone number, it just stuck in my head. I called you once before about two weeks ago. Your mother answered and said it was too late for you to come to the phone. It was ten o'clock, I didn't think that was so late."

"It is here."

"That's why I called early this time. Where do you go to school?"

"Jeff High. I'm a junior."

"A junior! How old are you, Cary?"

"I'll be seventeen in two months. How old are you?"

"Do I have to answer that?"

"What are you, really young? Twelve or something?"

"Twelve! I'm sixteen."

"That's not so bad. Pete, I have to hang up now, my fifteen minutes are up."

"What do you mean?"

"That's the limit on phone calls in our house."

"I never heard anything like that. What do they have, a timer on you? How about sixteen minutes? Do they cut the cord if you go over?"

"Sure, and then they lock me in the attic. I really have to hang up now, Pete—"

"Cary, wait. I want to see you again. I'll come look for you at Jeff—"

"You'll never find me, Pete, there's a thousand kids there. 'Bye, Pete, it's been fun."

"Cary! Cary Longstreet! Listen, don't go yet, I have to tell you something . . . I love you! Did you hear me? I'll probably never have the nerve to say it again. Cary? . . . Cary! Oh, well. You're going to be sorry you didn't hang on to hear that."

Fourteen

"Over here, Pete." Joanie Casson waved to me from the lunch line where she was standing with Drew. It had been raining steadily for hours and, for once, the cafeteria had business.

"Drew and I saw you this morning near the trophy case," Joanie said as I joined them. "You walked right by us, head in the clouds. Cosmic thoughts?" Joanie was probably the most artistic person in Winston High, loads of talent, her paintings were always winning prizes. She was probably also the thinnest person in the entire school. Really, it was strange looking at her with Drew: the twig and the tree.

"Ah, well, there's this girl—" I said.

"A girl?" Joanie said, loading her tray with food. Today was foot-long-hot-dog-with-oven-baked-beans day. Joanie took double helpings. "You have a girl friend, Pete?"

I checked out the tuna fish sandwiches for one with mayo dripping over the edges, the way I liked it. Did Joanie have to sound that surprised?

"Who is she?" Drew said. "Is she pretty?"

"Why do you always have to know right away if a girl is pretty?" Joanie said.

"I don't want my friend stuck with a dog."

"I really hate that kind of talk about girls! As if all that counts is their looks. It's dumb, Drew."

"I'm just teasing him, Joanie. What makes you so sensitive?"

"What makes you so insensitive?" She took her tray and walked away.

Drew shook a fist after Joanie. "I really love that girl, but sometimes I wonder. Who's your girl, someone I know?"

"She goes to Jefferson. Her name is Cary Longstreet."

We walked toward Joanie's table. "Maybe I should meet her," Drew said, loud enough for Joanie to hear, "especially if she's great-looking. I'll check her out for you."

Joanie leaned toward him and spoke quietly. "I bet Pete really appreciates your thoughtfulness—you turd."

Drew flushed. "You play rough, Joanie."

"You don't?"

We all ate in silence for a few minutes, then Joanie said, "You coming out to watch the game with Salem High after school, Pete? Drew's starting."

"Salem's no challenge for Drew. We're going to win, aren't we?" After school I was going nowhere but the Nut Shoppe.

"Even so," Joanie said. "I love watching Drew pitch. He's so good and sooo beautiful out there. Irresistible to an artist." She put her arm through his. "You over your mad? I'm over mine."

After school, I made the mistake of stopping in Gene's office to ask for a couple of bucks. The instant I stepped through the door, I became suddenly indispensable. "Oh, Pete, good," my uncle said. "We're all out of stamps and we're trying to get the billing done." He dipped a pair of frames into the hot salt solution and bent them carefully. "Mrs. Silk will tell you what we need at the post office. When you get back, you can help her stuff the envelopes. You don't have anything else to do, do you?" he added.

"Actually, I do."

"Well, this shouldn't take more than a few minutes."

Wrong. By the time I left the office, the few minutes had turned into a few hours and when I got to the Nut Shoppe, Cary was just leaving. "Closed for the night?" I said, coming up behind her.

She turned, looking startled, then smiled. "Oh, it's Pete Green Wood. *Quelle* coincidence."

"Just happen to be walking down this street on the way to see a friend," I said, falling into step with her.

"Again? And once more you're going the same way I am?"

"Amazing, isn't it?" We stopped on the corner and she leaned into the street, looking for the bus. "Are you going to be home tonight?" I said. "I was thinking of calling you. Is fifteen minutes really as long as you can stay on this phone?"

"That's the rule of the house."

"Your folks are pretty strict."

"Yes, they are, but that's okay, I don't mind. There are other compensations."

"Which are?"

"They're wonderful and loving, and that's really the most important thing in the world. At least I think so. Oh, here comes my bus."

"Cary," I said quickly, "how about doing something together Sunday? Maybe we could go for a bike ride—"

"You on my handlebars? No thanks, Green Wood."

"I have a bike too." I hadn't used the old blue charger for a couple of years, but it was waiting patiently for me in the back shed.

She shifted her books. "Anyway, I don't go out with boys. No boyfriends."

I started to laugh, then, seeing her expression, which was completely serious, I said, trying to sound truthful, "I don't want to be your boyfriend." And I added, "Are you one of those women who hate men?" It was just one of those jokey, offhand remarks. In Joanie's terms, a dumb thing to say.

"No," Cary said very softly, "but I might be . . . I really might be." And then something happened—her eyes didn't exactly go out of focus, but they changed, deepened, and her face changed too, and I had the sensation that she had left me, left the street, was absolutely somewhere else. It was exactly as strange and surprising a moment, and as powerful and almost shocking in its effect on me, as that moment in the Nut Shoppe, weeks ago, when the Princess had been transformed into a pleading little girl. And just like that moment, I saw this change happen, then saw it *un*happen.

The bus arrived and stood at the corner, dirty and wounded-looking, huffing out exhaust fumes. The crowd surged toward the door and Cary's eyes came back to the present. She went up the steps, taking out her token.

"Cary," I called. "Sunday? A friendly bike ride, okay?"

She looked over her shoulder. "I'll let you know. I have to talk to my mother."

All the way home I thought about Cary. There was something odd about her—not exactly strange, but— different. *Different.* That was the word that popped into my mind. Different? Wasn't that *me* to a tee? Me with my secrets, lies? *My name is Pete Greenwood. My parents are dead. I love baseball, doesn't every av-*

erage American boy love baseball? I sniffed the warm spring air, as if I could sniff out who Cary really was, and what that difference was in her, that difference that made me more eager than ever to know her.

Fifteen

*Two dark enormous figures ran down an alley where
I stood in a doorway. As they passed me, I realized
they were not only enormous but also as tiny as toy
soldiers. I knew they were looking for me, but they
passed right by me.*

I woke up with a cry. The sun came into the room
in bars through the venetian blinds. I lay in bed,
letting the dream go. It wasn't all that hard to figure
out.

"Pete?" Gene rapped on my door. "Fried eggs if
you get up right now."

"Okay." I rolled out of bed, yawning. Then I remembered Cary's phone call last night and did my
push-ups in record time.

"Can you come to my house Sunday around two
o'clock with your bike?" she'd asked.

"Then it's all set?"

"Not really. My parents want to meet you and ask
you some questions."

"Questions?" I said. "Like what?"

"I don't know exactly, Pete, just some stuff to
make sure they feel okay about us being friends."
She emphasized *friends.* "And, Pete, they're real

bears about punctuality, so make it as close to two as possible, okay?"

I hopped around the room, pulling on jeans and a striped tee-shirt. I'd never heard of Drew's getting the once-over from anybody's parents.

In the kitchen, I sat down across from Gene and heaped eggs on my plate. He asked me some stuff about school and if I wanted to go out to dinner with him and Martha, and then he started talking about *Charley's Aunt,* the play he was in.

"I don't know about the director on this play we're doing. This is her first play—"

"Uh uh uh, watch that sexist stuff, or I'll have to sic Drew's girl friend on you."

"What I want you to do is come to a rehearsal in a week or so, Pete, and tell me how my character is shaping up."

"I get the chance to criticize you legitimately?"

"My character, not me, wise guy. Brassett's the quintessential English serving man—extremely polite and extremely shrewd. It's that shrewdness I want to get across."

I mopped up the eggs with a piece of toast. "Okay if I bring a friend with me?" Instant flash: Cary sitting next to me in the darkened theater, head close to mine, saying respectfully, *Does your uncle always ask your advice?* "Drew?" Gene said. "Sure."

"Not Drew. It's, um, it's a girl. No funny remarks, please."

"Is that who you were on the phone with last night? I sort of caught that it wasn't Drew."

"We're going on a bike ride, Sunday. That is, if I get her parents' seal of approval. They're looking me over before they let her out with me. Her parents are mucho strict. I have a feeling if I pass inspection they're going to slap a hunk of red wax on my forehead. 'Certified Harmless.' "

In the living room the grandfather clock struck the half hour. "How old is this girl?"

"Her name's Cary. Almost seventeen. As a sort of parent, you want to give me any good advice on how to impress her parents with how trustworthy and up-standing I am?"

" 'To thine own self be true.' "

"That's the best you can do?"

"Hmmm. Okay, be polite, try to understand their point of view, and smile. There's nothing like a smile."

"You really think so?" I bared my teeth at my uncle. "What if they ask me about Laura and Hal?"

"Why would they? Anyway, you know what to say."

I dumped my dishes into the sink and followed him out to the hall. "I'm not exactly your normal all-American kid, am I? Sometimes I get the feeling it shows. Like pimples. Even if you tell yourself to act like you don't have them, everybody else can see the ugly little brutes."

"Pete, calm down. Just go see your girl friend and put all that other stuff out of your mind."

"Stuff? You mean Laura and Hal? My parents? Is that what you do? Just wipe them out of the old mind? Blank them out as if they didn't exist? That's just great. That's really great!" I was suddenly shouting.

Gene looked at me for a moment, then put on his jacket and went out the door. I stood there, breathing hard. What the hell was the matter with me? I ran after my uncle. "Gene!" I caught him on the street. "Forget I did that, will you? The maniac in me—" I held out my hands. "I'm sorry."

On Sunday, on the way to Cary's house, the gears on my bike were skipping and I had to stop several times to adjust them. Even so, I was there too early. I rode past the house. Was Cary watching from the window? I bent forward over the handlebars, wishing I had a helmet with a chin strap. I rode around the block five or six times, checking my watch every other minute. At exactly two o'clock, I was on the porch, ringing the bell.

Cary answered the door. "Hi." She looked different again, I guess because of her hair—it was pulled back into a ponytail. And this was the first time I'd seen her in shorts.

I followed her into the house, suddenly nervous and trying to remember Gene's advice. In the living room she said, "Sit down, Pete, I'll get Mom and Dad." I perched on the edge of an upholstered chair. Not for anything would I have sat back and messed up the cushion. Everything in that room was perfect. Not a thing out of place. The magazines on the coffee table were stacked with their edges ruler-straight, the couch was fat and smooth—had anything as vulgar as a behind ever been on it?—and even the curtains at the windows billowed out as stiffly as if they were at attention. Martha said that for two guys, Gene and I kept ourselves in a very civilized manner, but compared to this house, we lived like a couple of slobs.

A little girl in overalls, carrying a tin robot, wandered in. We looked at each other. I tried to think of something to say to her. I didn't know anything about kids. She started the conversation. "Zoooom, zoooom, zoooom."

"Zoooom, zoooom, zoooom," I agreed. She ran the robot lightly over the arm of the couch and gazed at me with round blue eyes. A moment later, Cary came in with her father and her mother, who was holding a baby over her shoulder. I jumped up and Cary introduced us.

"Pete." Her father was short with broad shoulders. He gave me a handshake I wasn't going to forget soon. "Right on time," he said, giving me another powerful hand squeeze.

"How's the weather outside?" Cary's mother said. She was the woman with bangs and glasses who'd tapped on the window, the one I'd thought was Cary's older sister. Her father didn't exactly look young enough to be Cary's brother, but he didn't look that old either. He had the same blue eyes as the little girl with the robot.

"Pretty baby, Mrs. Longstreet." I remembered my uncle's advice to be polite and smile a lot.

"Yancey," she said.

"Oh! Sorry." I should have remembered how they answered the phone. I puzzled again over the two names and decided, looking from Mr. Yancey to Cary, that maybe he was her stepfather. She certainly looked more like Mrs. Yancey; they both had brown eyes.

"Well," Mr. Yancey said, "what's this about a bike ride? Where do you plan to go? How long will it take?"

Cary's mother sat down on the couch. Mr. Yancey picked up the little girl in overalls and sat down too. "I don't know about your family," he said, "but in our house we have rules that we expect Cary to follow. No exceptions."

I nodded, trying to look like I really understood their point of view.

"Where do you live, Peter?" Mrs. Yancey said.

"Mooreland Avenue."

"Mooreland? Isn't that downtown?" Mr. Yancey said. "Or is there another Mooreland Avenue?"

"No, it's downtown. Off South."

"Well, right. I would have been surprised to hear there was a Mooreland Avenue I didn't know about.

I've lived and worked in Winston all my life and I know it like the back of my hand."

"Do you and your brothers and sisters like living downtown?" Mrs. Yancey said. "Don't you miss having a yard?"

"We do have a yard. Not very big, but we have a couple of trees. It's really nice. The house is old." That didn't sound good. "I don't mean old crappy—" I stopped again, realizing from Mrs. Yancey's face that I'd goofed. *Crappy* was a no-no. "The house is historical," I said quickly. "When my uncle bought it, he saved it from the wreckers."

Mrs. Yancey patted the baby. "Your uncle lives with your family? That's nice."

I cleared my throat. "Actually, it's just the two of us."

"Just you and your uncle? No sisters or brothers? How awful for you. And where are your parents?"

"My parents—" I cleared my throat again. "Actually, they're dead." As always when I said this, my lips went numb.

"Oh, I'm so sorry," Mrs. Yancey said. "I didn't mean to bring up a painful subject. I know how it feels to be alone." There was a short pause—for sympathy?—then Mrs. Yancey went briskly back to the subject at hand. Onward with the investigation of one Pete Greenwood. "Now what does your uncle do, Peter?"

"You mean for a living? He's an optometrist. Greenwood's Optometry Center. That's downtown too."

"I know the place," Mr. Yancey said. "Years ago there was a cigar shop right there. Where do you go to school?

"Winston High."

"On the other side of town. How old are you?"

"Sixteen."

"Sixteen," Mrs. Yancey repeated, with a little tuck of her mouth. "When I was sixteen, I was wild. I was a wild kid, so I know all about being sixteen."

She seemed to be waiting for me to say something. "Ah, I try not to be too wild." I glanced at Cary. Did I get a smile on that one?

"I hope you realize that Cary is not interested in having a boyfriend."

Cary spoke for the first time. "People can be just friends, Mom. It's not like when you were growing up."

Her mother brushed something off Cary's tee-shirt. "Certain things don't change, Cary. Boys are boys and girls are girls and that's the way life is."

"Maybe, but Pete and I are just friends."

"I want to count on that," Mr. Yancey said, fixing his blue eyes directly on me. "You may think we're a little strict, Pete, but our point of view is that there's nothing more important than watching out for our children's welfare."

I nodded. Cary pulled on a white hooded sweater. "Can we take some cookies and apples?" she asked. And I realized that, whatever the test was, I must have passed.

Sixteen

Outside Winston, the fields were bare, but the trees were starting to show some green. About a mile up a back road, my bike made an ominous rattling noise, then I found myself pedaling and going nowhere. I kicked the bike a couple of times to let it know what I thought of its treachery.

"What happened?" Carrie doubled back.

"Something's wrong with the gears. It was glitching up the whole way over to your house."

"Did you bring your tools?"

"No."

"I didn't take mine either. What a pain."

"The tools, the bike, or me? Never mind, answer me this question instead. If we go out for an ice cream cone, do your parents do the Spanish Inquisition bit? Or was that special treatment for a big event like this bike ride?"

"I don't want you to make cracks about my parents."

"It was just a joke."

"Well, I guess I don't like jokes like that."

In the distance, cows were grazing on the slopes. Cary took the food from her saddlebag. "Want something to eat while we figure out what to do with your bike?"

"Okay with me. Do you think we should let your parents know that we've changed our plans?" Me and my big mouth. "Sorry," I mumbled.

She nodded, but we sat there for quite a while without saying anything. Frowning and biting her lips, Cary folded and refolded a napkin into tiny squares, the little-girl look on her again. I began to feel exceptionally rotten, the way I did when I was mean to my uncle. "Sorry for that," I said again. "Forget I said it?"

She nodded and bit into an apple, but we still didn't seem to have anything to say to each other. I lay back on the ground, just this side of depressed. Here I'd gone through all that stuff to get the Yancey Good Boy Seal of Approval—and so what? Did Cary and I actually have anything in common? Was she really different? Did I truly have a special feeling for her? And what about her? Did she have *any* feeling at all for me?

A pickup truck approached, trailing a plume of dust. The driver stared at us as he passed slowly. Several guns were racked in the back window.

"I hate guns," Cary said.

"Me too," I said, glad to find something we agreed on.

After another moment, she said, "Want a cookie?"

"Thanks." I tried out a smile on her. "Your mother doesn't look much older than you."

"She isn't. She's twenty-six."

I laughed. "She had you when she was nine years old."

"I'm a foster."

"A foster?"

"A foster child. Mom and Dad are my foster parents. . . . You don't have to look so shocked."

"No, I'm not. It's just—I'm surprised. So that's

101

why your name is Longstreet and theirs is—I never thought—I didn't realize—"

"Why should you? I don't go around with a sign on, 'Beware the foster child.' "

"I never met a foster."

"Well, now you have."

"Why do you call your foster parents Mom and Dad?"

"Because they're my parents. Just like Kim and Jamie are my sister and brother. They're my family just as much as your uncle is your family."

"Are you the only one?"

"The only one what?"

"The only foster in the family?"

"At the moment, yes. Kim and Jamie are Mom and Dad's birth kids. Anything else you want to know?"

"Yes, actually, but I think I'm making you sort of mad—"

"I'm not mad. Go ahead, satisfy your curiosity."

"No, no, I can tell you really don't want to talk about it."

"Why? Do you think I'm ashamed?"

"No, I didn't mean that, Cary. It's just that you sounded really sort of hostile. I mean, it's interesting to me, but—"

"I'm glad I'm such an *interesting* specimen."

"Cary! Come on! I didn't mean it that way."

"No? So what exactly is so *interesting* about me?"

"I didn't mean you, per se. Your situation. For instance, I didn't know they let people as young as Mr. and Mrs. Yancey be foster parents to teenagers."

"Why not, if they're good parents?"

I flopped over on my stomach and watched a couple of sluggish ants crawling around. After a few minutes of intensely loud silence, I said, "Hey, I've got another question. Do you dislike me?"

"No."

"Come on, tell me straight."

"Would I be here with you if I disliked you?"

"I don't know. Would you?"

"Do you think I'm desperate? Why would I spend an afternoon with someone I disliked? Because you've got short hair and pants? I am not that kind of person!"

"I hope you do like me," I said after a few minutes, "because I like you a lot."

"Do you? You don't even know me. There are things about me—you might not be so keen to be my friend if you knew certain things."

"Oh, come on, that's ridiculous. Now I know you're a foster. Is that what you mean?"

"That's the beginning. Anyway, I've had friends like you who said, 'Oh, no, no, nothing could make me stay away from you.' And then they changed their tune."

"Great friends."

She shrugged. "The world is full of rats and skunks and you can't always tell just by looking." She had an odd smile on her face, half proud, half cynical. She gave me a long look. "Can I trust you?" Another searching look. "I tend to get very strong feelings about people, very fast. Either I trust them or I don't. And if I don't—there's usually a good reason, even if I don't know it at first."

"Well, what about me? What's your strong feeling about me?"

"Oh, you're a hard one to figure out. You come on so simple and normal—" She laughed. "I don't know, that's a crazy thing to say, I guess."

"Not so crazy. There are things about me—"

"Yesss." She drew out the word. "I think I should trust you, but—I hope I'm not wrong. Listen up, Pete. You want to hear my story?"

I hesitated for an instant, wondering if the deal was her story for mine, but she'd already started talking.

"I lived with my real mother until I was four, Pete. They were the four most wonderful, most beautiful years of my life. My mother used to read to me every night . . . sit me in her lap and brush my hair. Then she got sick. Too sick to take care of me and my sisters. So the county came and took us and put us each out with a different family."

"They couldn't keep you together?"

"There aren't many families who would want three at once. I lived with the Moroscos first. I was there six months and it was pretty good but for some reason they took me away from them and put me with another family. That was only for a few weeks, I hardly remember them. After that I lived with the Albrands until I was six. Then they moved away to Texas and right after I started first grade, I went to live with Papa and Mama DeAngelis. Seven years. I had seven years with them, I was their only child and they wanted to adopt me. But they were in their sixties, and the county said they were too old and sent me to another family."

She stopped for a moment, then went on evenly, "They sent me to the Waterstripes. I was with them for a year. And after them, I lived with the Hurleys. They thought I ate too much. Stingy people. I was always hungry there. Whenever I did something they didn't like, they'd take away my supper or my breakfast. Sometimes I got so many demerits I didn't eat for two or three days. So I ran away. I went to New York City. Big dirty ugly city. I was on the streets for a few days, I slept a couple of nights in the train station. I was just walking around wondering how I was going to get a meal and where I should sleep when a woman came up to me and started talking. She said she was from Father Ritter's Covenant House and did I have a place to stay. Did you ever hear of Covenant House?"

"Yes."

"Well, I'd never heard of it. But I decided I trusted her and I went along with her. I didn't know where I was going and I didn't much care at that point. I stayed at Covenant House for about two months. I didn't want to come back here, until my social worker promised I wouldn't have to live with the Hurleys. Right after I came back to Winston, I stayed in PCH—you know what that is?"

I shook my head. I wanted to say something, but everything I thought of seemed inadequate. *Rough life . . . you've had a hard time . . .* Did she need me to tell her that?

"Funny, you know about Covenant House, which is in New York City, but not about Pinewood Children's Home, which is right here in Winston. Lousy place, I hate it. I stayed there for about a month until my worker found me another family. They had six other foster kids. I thought, Well, what is this? Are these people greedy or what? But I liked them. I really wanted to stay with Mom and Dad Serio—"

"Why didn't you?"

She shrugged. "My social worker was satisfied, but one of their other foster daughters didn't like me. Venda. I'll never forget that girl. She couldn't keep her fists off me. She stole some of my jewelry, too. So, finally, my social worker said I could go live with the Yanceys. And here I am. The end for the moment."

Her face was pale and tense. She looked ready to cry. I touched her arm. "Cary—Cary—when my parents—I used to cry every night for my mother."

She stood up and swung her leg over her bike. "Listen, Pete, I don't need your pity. Yours or anybody else's. And let me tell you something else. I never cried for my mother. Never." She pedaled down the road and out of sight.

Gene and I were watching a TV show a few nights later when Cary called. "Hi, Pete? Is this a good time for you to talk?"

"Cary?" I carried the phone from the kitchen into the dining room and sat on the staircase, where I could look into the living room and watch the show. "Martha?" Gene said. I shook my head.

"About Sunday," Cary said. "I shouldn't have just gone off and left you. Did you get home okay?"

"I'm here."

"You're mad, and I don't blame you."

"Not mad exactly." I walked back into the kitchen with the phone. "It's just—hey, where do we stand? I like to know where I stand with people. You jumped down my throat a dozen times and at the end there—"

"I know, I know," she interrupted. "I got into this beastly mood."

"Well, I guess it was kind of a tense thing for you, telling me all that."

"That's no real excuse, although that's sweet of you. But I have to work on myself, I should be able to control my moods better."

Things started crackling after that. I guess we both felt better and we talked until her mother blew the whistle. Just before she hung up, I asked her to go to one of Gene's play rehearsals with me.

"Yes, sure, that sounds like fun."

As she said it, I heard a car door slam outside. And then footsteps, with that hollow sound they get at night. All at once I had the sensation that this had happened before in exactly the same way.

Hanging up the phone—no, not the phone, a micro-phone, yes, a microphone in a drive-in movie—and then hearing the car door slam and footsteps approaching. Then the man in the clerical collar opening the door of Gene's Volvo and beckoning me.

Three years ago. Autumn. Gene and I were in North Carolina, Hilton Head, at a drive-in movie. The last night of a vacation that Gene had dreamed up suddenly. Just decided one night at supper to close the office, take me out of school for a week and go see the beaches in North Carolina. No sooner said than done.

The beaches were great. We stayed in a motel and ate out every night in a different restaurant. On the last night, Gene said he wanted to see *Fantasia,* which was playing at a drive-in theater. "I saw it when I was a kid and I've always wanted to see it again." But I was bored and ready to leave at intermission. Gene said no, he wanted to stay through. He left to buy hot dogs and fries, and I hung up the mike.

A moment later I heard a car door slam, then footsteps. The back of my neck chilled, as if I knew what was going to happen before it happened.

A tall thin man, wearing a white collar turned around like a priest, bent into the car. "Hello, Pax." He handed me a box of popcorn and said he would bring me to my parents. He held my arm, not hard, but firmly. We walked across the lot to another car. Laura and Hal were inside. This time I knew them.

We all sat tightly together in the front seat and ate popcorn. It was soggy and it stuck in my teeth. The movie came back on and an elephant danced on the screen. Laura and Hal asked me questions. *Are you eating? Do you sleep all right? How about school? Do you get along with Uncle Gene?* And all the time their eyes swiveled back and forth, looking out the windows and into the mirrors and out the windows again.

There was a pain in my chest that ran like a burrowing mouse into my stomach. I started begging them. I wanted to be brave, but I couldn't help myself. *Take me with you. I won't be any trouble. I'm old enough. I'm thirteen. I can be helpful. Take me with you.*

Hal hugged me. *Keep the faith.*

Laura kissed me and kissed me. *Soon, soon, we'll all be together again.*

"Pete?" Abruptly I became aware that Cary was still on the phone. "I have to hang up now. Let me know about that play rehearsal."

Outside, the footsteps slowly receded.

Seventeen

"Now where exactly is this place you want to go to with Cary?" her foster mother said. She cut a peach into sections and handed Cary a slice.

"The old Temple Beth El on Water Street," I said. "The Winston Theatre Guild took over the building a few years ago and they do everything there. All their rehearsals and then when they're ready to open the show—"

"That's a Jewish church, isn't it?"

"They don't use it as a synagogue anymore."

Cary leaned on her foster mother, not saying anything, just a little smile now and then for me as the questions flew thick and fast.

"There were a few little details Cary was unclear on. Give me the plan again. What's going on, how you're getting there, and what time I can expect Cary home?"

"My uncle Gene's rehearsing for a play. It's called *Charley's Aunt.* You've probably seen the movie, it's always on the late show with Ray Bolger—"

"Ray Bolger? He's the scarecrow in *The Wizard of Oz,* isn't he? We watch that every year."

"Rehearsal should be over around ten o'clock," I said.

"Too late. I want you home by ten, Cary. That's

late enough for a school night." Cary nodded and Mrs. Yancey turned back to me. "I know you don't live in this neighborhood, Peter, but I hope you're planning to see Cary back here."

"Yes, sure." Since, according to the Yancey Rules of Conduct I could not be Cary's boyfriend, but only Cary's friend who was a boy, I had half-expected to be told that I couldn't come back to the house with her.

"Does your uncle have a car?"

"Yes, a Volvo."

"Do you drive?"

"I had my permit, but I never took the test." Now she'd want to know why. Fear of failure? Too stupid to pass?

"Good, because we don't like Cary to go out in cars, especially with teenage drivers."

I glanced at Cary. Didn't it bother her at all that her foster mother talked about her as if she were closer to seven than seventeen?

"At your age," Mrs. Yancey said, "I did everything wrong, believe me. I was on my way to being one truly messed-up kid. My problem was I didn't have enough discipline at home. I'm not letting that happen around here. I tell Cary, you can holler and yell all you want, but when you're my age you'll look back and say, Now she had the right idea!" She hugged Cary. "Okay, go on and have a good time for yourself."

Outside, it was a warm overcast night. We waited at the corner for the downtown bus. Across the street, a pink neon sign on a restaurant flickered on and off.

"I'm in such a good mood," Cary said, when we got on the bus. "You don't have to worry that I'll go off and leave you tonight." She looked at me and laughed. "Just before you came, my mother and I

110

were talking, and she hinted really strongly that she and my father are going to give me a very special birthday present. You know what I think it is?" She leaned toward me. "They're going to adopt me!"

"Really?" I was surprised that at her age she still wanted to be adopted and even more surprised that people would adopt a teenager. "I always thought adoption was for little kids."

"Well, you thought wrong," she said. I could tell that she was annoyed by my remarks. "Some people even adopt people in their twenties or thirties."

"Oh." That seemed sort of bizarre to me, but this time I kept my mouth shut.

Rehearsal was already under way when we arrived. We took seats in back of the darkened theater. Martha was there, and I whispered introductions. The stage was full of people. "That's my uncle," I said, pointing. "The one in the striped—"

Someone clapped loudly. "Quiet back there, please!" Cary and I looked at each other and she squeezed my hand. A small woman in a black sweater and jeans ran up the stage. "Now, Lord Fancourt, let's stop and talk out this scene. What I want you to do on your entrance—"

"This is so neat," Cary whispered.

Later, the director called a break. "Why don't you take Cary backstage?" Martha suggested. "Tell Gene I'll be waiting for him when he's done, okay?"

Backstage, I introduced Cary to my uncle. "Delighted to meet you, young lady," Gene said, going courtly on us. "Are you enjoying the rehearsal?"

"I think you're terrific, Mr. Greenwood."

"Well, thank you!" He gave Cary a big smile. "How'd my accent strike you, Cary? Honestly, now."

"Excellent. It was so real."

"I primed her for that answer, Gene. I told her you lapped up flattery like a cat in the cream."

"Pete, you did not!"

Gene winked at her. "Don't worry, I live with this scoundrel, I know all his tricks."

I kept waiting for him to ask my opinion on how his character, Brassett, was shaping up. I had my answer ready and, naturally, I hoped it would impress Cary. But Gene seemed to have forgotten all about asking my advice. It was Cary this, Cary that.

"Now, did you notice that bit with the dustcloth, Cary—"

"Hold it, Uncle G," I interrupted on about the fifth question. "It's time for us to go."

"Already?" Cary said.

"Come on, you know if you're not home by ten o'clock, you turn into a pumpkin." Oops. I wasn't supposed to say things like that. Oh, well—I was feeling too good to feel bad.

"You're lucky," Cary said, as we walked toward the bus stop. "Your uncle is really nice."

"I see that you go for these good-looking, slightly overweight, elderly types."

"Your uncle's not old."

"Right next to Methusela."

She laughed. And, oh, how I wanted to kiss her; I'd been thinking about it all evening. Should I just—*do it?* Should I put my arms around her first? What about the no-boyfriends rule? She probably needed a signed application from me, swearing that it would be just a kiss between friends.

To Whom It May Concern: I, Pete Connors, the undersigned, herinafter known as The Friendly Kisser, do solemnly swear that I have no evil, lewd intentions toward Cary Longstreet, hereinafter known as The Friendly Kissee. The Friendly Kisser herein certifies that The Kiss will be a Genuine Friendly Kiss, to be returned in like manner by The Friendly Kissee. . . .

I didn't want a friendly kiss. I wanted the real Mc-

Coy, a kiss that would make her cheeks burn and my ears smoke. We walked along and I just kept thinking about it. Suddenly I leaned toward her, aimed for her lips, and landed on the corner of her mouth.

"Oh, Pete. Like this." She took hold of me by the ears and kissed me long and soft on the mouth.

Eighteen

A clap of thunder shook the window of the Nut Shoppe just as I walked in. "Hi! Got room on the ark here?" Cary was in back of the store, emptying a tin into one of the nut bins.

"How you'd get here so fast? I've just been here five minutes myself." She put the tin down and we smiled at each other.

"Ran all the way. How're you doing?"

"Good. How about you?"

"Same." Not a very exciting conversation, but I loved it.

All of a sudden, the sky darkened and the rain came, drumming against the window and door. Outside, people ran past with newspapers and briefcases over their heads.

A streak of green lightning forked down the middle of the street. "Did you see that?" Cary said. Thunder shook the windows again, the lights flickered, and the peanut-roasting machine stopped. Cary turned off the gas on the machine. There was a moment of eerie silence, then another flash of green lit the sky, and the lights went out.

"There's a fuse box in back," Cary said. In the dark, we fumbled toward the back room. "Ouch!" she yelled. She must have run into something. A moment later, we collided. "Oh, sorry," she said, "I can't see a thing."

"That was terrible. Uh, I'm hurt. Uh, uh." I groaned and groped hopefully toward her, but she was already past me.

"I can't find a fuse," she said. "See if you can find one, will you?"

"Negative."

"Great. I bet Mr. Blutter will find a way to blame me for that, too."

"Blutter? As in Blutternut?"

"Blutter, as in raging bull. If you knew that man—I cringe every time he comes in here. He doesn't know what it means to talk like a human being. Last week he popped in to tell me—excuse me! I mean *yell* at me about a few million things I was doing wrong. I went home shaking."

We went back into the shop where there was some light from the street. "Why don't you get another job?" I said.

"Think they grow on trees? I did housework before this, and even with Mr. Blutter, this is better. I really hated cleaning other people's messes."

"Why'd you do it then?"

"Same reason I stay on this job."

"Doesn't the county social services department, or whatever they call them, pay for things for you?" I said.

"Sure, basic stuff. Room, board, clothes—sort of— and medical bills. If I want anything extra, it's up to me. Mom and Dad don't have a lot of money either, you know. Do you get an allowance? I bet your uncle is really generous."

"Well, he is, but I work for my money too," I said, a little defensively. Obviously, my working for Gene was a whole lot different from Cary's working for Mr. Blutter.

We peered out the window. The whole street was dark. Rain poured down in hard gray sheets. There wasn't a soul in sight. "You know what," I said, "a fuse wouldn't do you any good anyway. The whole area's down. It's probably a transformer."

"That's what I was just thinking. I better call darling Mr. Blutter and let him in on the good news."

"No power?" I could hear him as clearly as if he were bellowing in my ear. "Close up! I'm not paying you for time you don't work. Close up!"

Cary banged down the phone. "How am I supposed to close up in the dark? He has fits if I miss a millimeter of a peanut when I sweep."

"I'll help you. Where's the broom?"

By the time we were finished the rain had let up, but there still weren't any lights on. I wasn't eager to leave. It was cozy being in the dark store together. "Why don't we hang out here for a while?"

"Are you kidding? I shouldn't have let you stay this long. If Mr. Blutter ever found out I had a friend here—" She drew her finger across her throat.

"Let's go to my house, then. It's just a couple of blocks away."

"I don't think so, Pete. My mother has fits if I don't come home on time."

"Cary, are they your parents or your keepers?"

"Look, Pete, *they love me.* When people love you, they don't let you just run wild."

I heard Mrs. Yancey in those words. I could have argued the point—was coming home a few minutes late now and then running wild? But I bit my tongue—I'd already said enough, and upsetting Cary was definitely not my first mission in life.

But a moment later she peered at her watch and said, "Actually, I have an hour—if I don't miss the bus . . ."

"You won't," I said. "I promise you won't."

116

Nineteen

Our house is tucked, or maybe squeezed is more accurate, between a couple of big office buildings while, at the same time, it is set quite far back from the sidewalk. "I never noticed this house," Cary said. "All the times I've been down this street—"

"You're not the first one." I unlocked the door and held it open for her. "Nobody expects to see a house downtown, so they don't. Want something to eat?"

"Not now. Is it okay if I look around?"

I trailed after her as she went from room to room downstairs, looking at everything. I don't think she missed a thing. I wouldn't have been surprised if she'd opened the refrigerator and taken inventory. In the living room she examined every picture on the wall.

"I know, I'm terrible," she said. "I'm fascinated by other people's houses. Every time I baby-sit for someone new, I have to roam through their entire house. Who are these people? Relatives?"

"That's my uncle's shrine. They're actors, writers, directors—people in the theater that Gene admires."

"Here's Joanne Woodward. Does he know her?"

"Doesn't he wish. He thinks she's great, even if she is in the movies now."

"What's wrong with the movies?"

"Nothing, but Gene's a theater snob, he thinks all the real actors are on a stage."

"Who's this black man?"

"Paul Robeson. He's dead now. He was a great actor, with a fantastic singing voice. He was one of these super people. Phi Beta Kappa in college, All-American in football, that sort of stuff. That one's Laurette Taylor, she's dead too. Gene saw her a million years ago on Broadway in a Tennessee Williams play. She was a drinker and falling apart, but he says she was still a superb actress. He was only a kid then, but he was pretty stagestruck and he got her autograph after the show."

"Do you know everything about all these people?"

"No," I said, but Cary went from picture to picture anyway, asking for details, and I told her whatever I knew. I was surprised how many of Gene's stories had stuck with me.

I got us both soft drinks and Cary said, "I might as well see everything. What's upstairs?"

"Not that much. Just our bedrooms."

On the way up, Cary stopped to look at one of Martha's watercolors that was hanging in the stairwell, an old willow tree growing over a stream, and in the background a faded red barn. "This is beautiful. Did someone famous paint this?"

"Martha. She has a little place downtown."

Cary continued up the stairs. She peeked into Gene's room, into the tiny spare room that was really a walk-in closet with a window, and even into the bathroom. "What a neat bathtub!"

"Gene goes for old-fashioned stuff. This is my room—" I opened the door. "Excuse the mess, I didn't know I was going to have company." I swooped up a bunch of dirty clothes and shoved them into the closet.

"Is this your shrine?" she said, looking at the Koren cartoons I had on the wall.

"No, not the way the pictures downstairs are Gene's shrine. I could never be a cartoonist, but I think this guy is a genius. He just makes me break out laughing." I watched hopefully as she read each caption, looked up at the picture, then down at the caption again. The best Koren got out of her was one very small smile. Oh, well . . . nobody's perfect.

"I love this slanted ceiling," she said. "This house is really wonderful." She took a hairbrush out of her pocketbook and started brushing her hair.

If I tried to kiss her here, would she think I was trying for a lot more? I perched on the windowsill. I liked the way Cary did everything—the sober little look she gave herself in the mirror, the neat way she put her brush back into her pocketbook, even the way she checked out each book on the table next to my bed. I guess, at that moment, she could have done anything at all and I would have thought it was fantastic.

She gave the rocker a little push, then sat down in front of my desk. It's a small rolltop with lots of little drawers and cubbyholes. She opened and shut one drawer after another. "Where'd you get this desk? It must be a real antique."

"I think it is. Gene got it for me a couple of years ago."

"For your birthday?"

"No, just—he found it in an antique shop and he thought I'd like it."

"He really is sweet, isn't he?" She picked up a notebook. I watched her do it without a twinge of alarm. I was still in the dream of her being in my room.

"What's this for?" she said. "What are all these numbers?" She had my license plate notebook.

119

I jumped up. "It's nothing. Give it to me."

"Uh, uh, uh, it is, too, something. Your face is turning red." She studied a page. "Now what is this? A code or something? Oh, I get it! It's love letters in code! SWW158. Who's she? No, no, no, don't tell me, let me guess. Sally Wilson Wade. But why is Sally in the NOTED section? Does that mean she noted you or you noted her? And who's this? 706AAG. DEFINITE. My, my, my. Definite what? Definite love? Pete! With a name like that? Hope you gave her up. She sounds like a disaster."

I reached for the notebook, but Cary held it over her head.

"Cary, come on."

She ducked under my arm, mimicking me. " 'Cary, come on!' . . . Tell me how to break this code and I'll give it to you."

I sat down on the bed and covered my face. I could never explain the notebook. *My hobby is memorizing the license plates of cars I think are following me.*

After a moment, she sat down next to me. "Pete— did I make you mad or something? I was just teasing." She tossed the notebook into my lap. "Was I really mean?"

"No, it's just—" I didn't know what to say. "Can I kiss you?" I blurted.

Her hair smelled like peanuts and rain. I never wanted to stop kissing her, or go away from her, or let her go away from me. We had our arms around each other, I couldn't get close enough, I wanted more . . . more . . . more . . .

Suddenly she pulled away, moved away from me, her face freezing into the Princess mask. "Look," she said, "just because we kissed—just because I came here, you don't have to think— How about me? How about what I want?"

I sat there, dumb and aching, shook my head,

couldn't speak. I didn't want her to look at me that way. I thought, What if I told her about my parents? I'd often imagined telling someone, just spilling it all out—to Drew, or his sister Deirdre, or Totie Golden. Totie would want to know, wouldn't she? It was history in the stream, not along the banks. Once or twice, in a strange reckless mood, almost as though I were sleeping on my feet, I had even thought of collaring a stranger on the street. *Listen! I have to tell you something important . . . secret . . . I don't do this lightly. Pay attention! My secret is going to be your secret.*

"Cat got your tongue, Pete? Hey—" Cary touched my head. "It's not that bad."

Cary, my parents are not dead. They're fugitives from the law . . . political outlaws. . . .

"What are you mumbling about?"

"My parents—my parents—"

She bent toward me. "Pete, are you okay?"

"My parents . . . Cary, they're in hiding . . ."

What had I said? What had I done? I'd never told anyone. I seemed to stop breathing. Everything in me froze. I had given away my parents, betrayed them. Suddenly I saw them hunched together in a dark closet. Safely hidden . . . until someone told on them. *Me.* My stomach did that lurching, grabbing thing. I yanked the closet door open, they tumbled out. Then I saw them in a car, driving through barren lands, miles of deserted desert. Outlaws . . . on the lam. My mother was a lamb . . . fierce lamb who had left a bomb in a wastebasket . . . and my father was a friendly frog with bulging green eyes and a great and glorious smile.

"What? What did you say?"

They bombed a lab, Cary; it wasn't an act of terrorism, but of conscience.

"Hey, you're sweating like anything."

The lab was doing germ warfare research. Hal and Laura wanted to bring it into the open, bring the truth to everyone.

She put her hand on my forehead. "You're really burning. I think you're getting sick."

The action was planned so the bomb would detonate when no one was there. Those two people—no, I don't want to talk about it. . . . They weren't supposed to be there. Laura and Hal wouldn't hurt a fly, that's no joke, our house was a safety zone for flies . . .

From across the street, we heard the bells in St. Luke's chiming the hour. Cary jumped up. "Pete, I should have left ages ago."

I followed her down the stairs. She hadn't heard me. She hadn't heard me! Outside, big ragged clouds raced through the sky. A sign banged against a post. I walked with her to the bus stop, dazed by what I'd almost told her, as dazed as if I'd had walked in front of a speeding car and only by a miracle missed being hit.

That night I dreamed I was walking down a dark alley with a little kid riding my back, his arms choked around my neck. "Too hard! Too hard!" I yelled, but when I looked around, it was a squirrel on my shoulder. He bit deep into my ear. I screamed with pain. A moment later, I was in a high cool room being questioned by someone I couldn't see.

Do you swear to tell the truth, the whole truth and nothing but the truth sohelpyouGod?

I do.

What is your name?

Pete Greenwood.

Liar. Your name?

Pete Greenwood.

Your name.

Pete Greenwood!

Take him away.

No! Wait!
Take him away.

I woke up moaning, in the grip of the White Terror, choking for air, faceless, empty. A breeze blew through the venetian blinds and I rocked in the terror, sweating and holding on to myself until it passed.

And when it was gone, I fell limply over the side of my bed and saw the notebook where I'd dropped it on the floor. I picked it up. The fresh odor of Cary's hair rose faintly from the pages. I rolled back on the bed, holding the notebook against my chest.

Twenty

As I left the house for school, two men emerged from a blue car parked across the street and strolled toward me. One was tall, one short. Both were well-dressed but casual. The tall one had a jacket slung over his shoulder. The shorter one flashed a black leather card case with an official stamp at me. "Pax Connors?" he said pleasantly. "Can we talk to you for a few minutes?"

My heart thudded, my eyes fuzzed over. After all these years, *they* had found me, tracked me down like dogs after a rabbit. And like a rabbit, I wanted to dive for cover. I looked this way, that way; my stomach was watery, but the hounds were on either side of me, smiling their doggy smiles.

"I don't have to talk to you." How many times had my parents impressed that on me? *You never have to talk to them. You don't have to tell them anything, not even the time of day.*

"I'm Frank Miner," the short investigator said, in the same pleasant tone, "and my partner here is Jay Beckman. You on your way to school, Pax? We won't hold you up too long. Jay and I just want to talk to you for a few minutes. No big deal. Just a little chat."

"My name is Pete," I said, "Pete Greenwood."

Why had I said it? I didn't have to talk to them. I didn't have to tell them anything, not even the time of day.

The taller one, Jay Beckman, gave me a knowing smile. "So, *Pete,* tell me, have you heard from Laura and Hal recently?"

"I don't know what you're talking about." My lips felt peculiarly stiff.

Frank Miner put his hand on my arm like a fond uncle. "Oh, sure you do, kid. Look, let's put all that crappadappa aside. You're Pax Connors, Laura and Hal are your folks, you know it and we know it. Hey! You know we've been looking for you for quite a while." He chuckled, a merry sound, as if their looking for me had been nothing but a game, Hide-and-Seek on a spring night, and I was It, and wasn't I the hell of a little devil to find such a terrific hidey-hole?

"So here we are," he went on, "and all we want to do is talk to you. No sweat. Say, are you okay? You look a little off—maybe we should go get something to eat, all of us. What about it, Jay? You drink coffee, Pax?"

I shook my head.

"Good," Frank Miner said. "Coffee's a bad habit. I don't let my kids drink it." Without my noticing, they had begun walking, one on either side of me. "I have a son just about your age," Frank Miner went on. "Nice kid, you'd like him, you two would probably get along. Don't you think so, Jay?"

Jay shrugged. He was the silent one, the tough one.

"Don't worry about school, you can be a little late," Frank Miner said. "We'll make it okay with the principal. I'll bet you're a good student. You're a smart kid. I read that you've got a high IQ. Do you get on the honor roll all the time? My kid works his butt off and never makes it. I don't know who's more

125

disappointed, me or him. He wants to be a lawyer and an investigative agent like the old man. Well, I tell him, you need the marks. So what are you thinking about doing after you're through high school, Pax? Oh, sorry, I guess you'd rather we called you Pete."

Read about me? Where did he read about me? What did that mean? Did they have a dossier on me? I stared around me as if I'd never seen these streets before. We passed stores I'd been into thousands of times, the Winston Savings Bank, Winston Square, the post office. How much did they know about me? Did they know about my place down in that little woods behind the post office? Did they know about Cary? Why was I walking like a sheep between the two of them?

"These years must have been hard on you, kid," Frank Miner said, turning to look right into my eyes. "Eight years without your old man or your mama— that's tough," he said, sounding so sympathetic the breath went out of me as if someone had whacked me with a bat between the shoulder blades. And a flood of words rose into my throat: I might have told them everything then, spilled it all without restraint.

"I can feel for you, Pete, not just abstractly," Frank Miner went on. "My father was gone for a couple of years—not my fault. Definitely not. He was a miner— yeah, he really was. Our name is Miner and he was a miner. But the name didn't do us any good. The coal fields were down, there was no work for him. My old man couldn't move the whole family, didn't have the money, so he took off to find a job. He did it for us, right? But let me tell you, I missed him. I missed my father." He squeezed my arm. "I still choke up, just thinking about it."

"Frank," Jay Beckman cut in, "we have some

business to do here. Let's get off that old family stuff. Nobody wants to hear about that."

We walked on without speaking. There was a numbness across the back of my head. I had stopped thinking, was simply walking—or was I being led?

"This looks like a good spot," Frank Miner said, stopping in front of a diner painted in rainbow stripes. "You know this place, Pete? Rainbow Diner? I could go for a stack of pancakes right now. How about you?" He held the door open.

I didn't move.

"Let's go, kid." Jay Beckman gripped my arm.

I walked into the diner between them, compliant, will-less, numbed by that urge to blab, to tell everything. Wouldn't it be a relief? At last, to get it all out of my mind, to empty all the little secret places, to pour out the accumulated debris of eight years—the grief, the anger, the notebooks, the license plates, the fears, the meetings, the hopes, the disappointments, the waiting, always the waiting . . . all of it, all of it. I only had to begin.

Eight years ago, a man I called Uncle Marti told me my parents had to go away for a while . . .

Good boy, good boy. They'd pat me on the head and feed me a doggie biscuit as I blatted everything out, as I gave them all the information they wanted and along the way betrayed my parents to the enemy.

Frank Miner sat down in one of the scratchy little red vinyl booths. "Sit down, kid. Breakfast's on me."

"I—I—" I stuttered and then, afraid of myself, terrified of my need to talk, twisted out of Jay's grip and ran out of the diner.

"Hey, kid!" Frank called after me. "Pete—come on back."

I ran and kept running and didn't stop until I was in school.

127

Twenty-one

"You going to eat that turkey sandwich?" Drew said.

"It's all yours." We were sitting in the bleachers near the playing field. I had no appetite. Ever since I'd run out of the diner that morning, my stomach had been churning.

"Joanie was over to the house last night." He ate the sandwich fast and crammed a cupcake into his mouth. "She gave me back my class ring. Threw it at me, threw it right at me." Suddenly he stood up and shouted at a couple of guys out on the field, who were tossing a ball back and forth. "Get your arm into it, Matheson, you dumb ass!"

He was quiet for a moment, then burst out, "You know what Joanie said? 'I'm fed up with sharing you with a dozen other girls. I can't believe anything you say!' Hell! I never lied to her. My hand to God. My mom and Dawn were downstairs in the shop, but Deirdre heard everything . . . my adorable sister. She said I bloody got what I bloody deserved. What am I supposed to do now, Pete?"

"You mean about Joanie?"

"What else, man! Are you listening or not?"

"I'm listening, I'm listening." But I was thinking about the agents.

"I tried to give Joanie back the ring this morning. She wouldn't take it, she wouldn't talk to me . . ."

"God, Drew, I don't know what to tell you. What I know about girls—"

"You've got a girl friend now. Are you having problems with her? I know you're not, because you don't have crazy girls calling you up and screwing things up for you."

"Why don't you disconnect your phone?"

"I really appreciate that advice, Greenwood. Try again."

"That's what you have to do. Try again. You never know till you try. Don't give up so easily, Gregoretti." The old clichés poured out like water from a faucet.

"Maybe you're right."

"Way to go." I sank back against the bleacher. What had I said this morning? Had I said anything I shouldn't have? What I remembered most distinctly were their names and their faces. Jay Beckman. Hollywood hatchet face. Frank Miner. Friendly-eyed as a dog.

Later that afternoon, not far from school, I saw a blue car with two men in it. I turned into the nearest store, walked through and out the back door. I took a different route home. But then, near the Interstate loop, I saw a man standing at a window on about the fourth floor in the Flannagan Building, staring straight down at me. One of *them*. Later I asked myself, Why would they put an agent in a building that they couldn't possibly have known I was going to pass? The answer was—they wouldn't. But at that moment, fear was stronger than logic. I ducked out of sight, my stomach churning again.

The worst moment came when I stopped in a market to buy milk. As I reached into the cooler, a man brushed briskly past me. Frank Miner! I must have groaned. He turned and looked at me for a moment. He was younger than the agent, shorter, fatter. Didn't look like him at all.

By the time I got home, I'd worn myself out seeing agents on every corner. I turned on the TV, then turned it off, then turned it on again. I couldn't think, couldn't make up my mind about anything. Should I tell Gene? I needed support. But why worry him? Well, he should know. Still, wasn't it my problem? I went round and round, but when Gene walked in, I stopped thinking and blurted it out.

"They've found me, Gene, they were waiting for me this morning when I left the house."

He went into the kitchen and filled the teapot.

"Agents, Gene. Two agents. They called me by my real name. They were parked across the street, a blue car, but then they left it and just walked with me." Why wasn't he jumping up and down? How about a little reaction? Some fear and panic, to keep me company if nothing else. "Did you hear me? Did you hear what I said?"

He poured boiling water into the teapot. "Of course, I heard you." His voice was as even as usual. "What exactly did they ask you, Pete?"

"They just said they wanted to talk to me. The short one, Frank Miner, he was chatty, pretty nice, but the tall one—the way he looked at me—real cold blue eyes, and tough. He asked me when I'd heard from Laura and Hal. And the way he said their names—"

Gene carried his tea into the dining room. "So they've found us." He sat down, took a sip of his tea, then got up and pulled down all the window shades, even though it was still light outside. That was the first sign I had that he was disturbed. He peered around the drawn shade. "Did you say a blue car?"

My heart jumped. "Are they out there?"

"No . . . no . . . just the usual traffic." He looked at me. "This morning?" he said, as if he were only now beginning to understand. He sat down close to me and whispered, as if Miner and Beckman were crouched under the plank table, taking down every word. "I used to worry about it all the time, that they'd connect me to Laura, come for you . . . I knew it was an advantage that I had a different last name than Laura, but still I worried. Do you think they knew all along and were just waiting . . . but for what? Why now? Jesus. What are they going to do, come around and grill us all? Me, Martha—"

"Martha doesn't know anything, she doesn't know about me."

"That's right, she's not involved. And for that matter, what could they find out from me? I know nothing about Laura and Hal's politics except what I read in the paper, the same as anybody else."

He got up and started walking around. "I still remember reading about that explosion in the lab and thinking it was just one of those awful things, a tragedy, a freak accident . . . that's what the newspapers said at first. And then later that day or the next day the news came out, a bomb had been planted and two people—"

I pushed away from the table, scraping the chair legs across the floor. "Why bring this up now? What good is that? We have to think, not chew over the past like a couple of cows."

"So it just happened this morning?" he said again. And then, going back to the past, driving me mad with his meanderings, he said in that same melancholy, perplexed voice, "When you first came to me, every time a stranger walked into the office, I thought, Uh huh! Here we go. I knew just what I was going to say to them. 'Look, I don't know anything about my sister's politics. That's not my thing in

131

life.' I had an entire speech. I used to practice—gestures, everything. But no one bothered us. And a year passed and another year, and I thought, Okay, that's it. Right. They're not coming." He frowned. "Pete, are you sure they were who they said they were?"

"Who else would they be? Who else would know my real name? Pax, they said. Pax Connors."

"Did you have a good look at their identification?"

"No," I said reluctantly. Frank Miner had flashed his card in front of my eyes—now you see it, now you don't—and I hadn't had the presence of mind to ask to look at his ID again. "He opened his wallet or card case, whatever it was, showed it to me, and put it away before I could check it out."

"Just like TV," Gene said. "Just like TV." For some reason, the way he said it struck both our funny bones. We started laughing, laughing so hard we couldn't stop. Every time our eyes met, we started all over again.

"Now I mean it this time," Gene said sternly. "I am stopping. This is no laughing matter." We pounded our fists on the table and laughed as hysterically as two little kids.

Twenty-two

Early the next morning, Gene came into my room and sat down on the edge of the bed. He was still in his pajamas. I had been lying in bed, half awake, for a long time. "Tell me again what happened with those two guys," Gene said.

Yawning, I leaned up on my elbow. Last night, after our laughing fit, we had talked for hours but, oddly, not about the agents at all. Somehow I got going on my love of history and, to my surprise, Gene had been really enthusiastic. In two seconds he'd had me through college and in graduate school, working for a combined master's and doctorate.

"Did I tell you I thought I'd seen their car before?" I yawned again, my eyes tearing. "Last week, a few times—only I thought I was being paranoid."

"Why didn't you tell me?"

I got out of bed and pulled on my jeans. "If I told you all the times I thought someone was watching me—" I picked up my notebook, hesitated for a moment, then handed it to him. "This is a record I've kept of of license plates and cars—"

Gene flipped through the notebook. "Good Lord, Pete. I had no idea you'd been worrying about these things."

"What difference would it have made, Gene? I'm a

little crazy anyway, I don't think you can change that."

"But that you've felt so insecure . . . and I didn't have a clue. Are there other things like this you've kept to yourself?"

What if I told him about the dreams of headless bodies . . . the White Terror . . . waking up in a panic . . . I leaned into the mirror and that dizzying white nothingness touched me. With an effort, I pulled myself out of the swaying moment of sickness. "I'm hungry," I said. "You making breakfast this morning?"

We went downstairs. Gene decided to make oatmeal. "I need something hot this morning. Pete, do you think anybody saw you with those men?"

I spooned peanut butter out of the jar. "There's not that many people out that early around here."

"I didn't sleep half the night thinking about this business."

"What were you thinking?"

"Oh . . ." Gene sighed, then busied himself punching holes in his cereal. When he had enough holes, he sprinkled in raisins, poured in milk and pushed each raisin into a puddle of milk to plump it up. When I was little, I used to love watching him fix his hot cereal.

"I didn't think anything startling," he said finally, "but I came to some conclusions. Number one." He held up one finger. "Okay, so they know you're here. Nothing we can do about that. Number two." Up went another finger. "We shouldn't panic. They obviously want information about Laura and Hal, but what can either of us possibly tell them? You've lived here for eight years. You've hardly seen your folks. You can't give these guys information you don't have and neither can I."

"Wait a second, wait a second," I said, putting my

milk down so abruptly it slopped onto the table. "Even if I did have information, do you think I'd tell it to them? They're gunning for my parents. I already made a big mistake answering any of their questions. I shouldn't have talked to them at all. I didn't have to say anything to them, and in the future, believe me, I'm not going to."

Gene reached over to the sink for the sponge. "It's okay to be principled," he said slowly, sponging up the milk. "I understand what you're saying and I sympathize. You certainly don't want to be put in the position of saying anything that could hurt your parents." He wrung the sponge out in the sink and sat down again. "However, as far as I'm concerned, if they come to me, what's the harm in saying, 'I don't know anything. I have no information for you guys—' "

"But, Gene," I interrupted, "that's not exactly true. What about that time I saw Laura and Hal in North Carolina? And what about when Marti came for me? What if they know about that stuff? What if they ask you about all that? If you're saying you'd talk if you knew anything, then the logic is that you do have to tell what you know. And once you start telling even a little bit, where do you stop?"

Gene flushed. "I hardly spoke to that Marti character, I wasn't impressed with him. As for the other time—all I did was take you to the drive-in and then leave the car."

"But someone must have gotten in touch with you. We went on that vacation all of a sudden. It wasn't even a school vacation."

Gene pushed aside his cereal bowl. "We had a good time, didn't we? Remember the drive down?"

"No. What I remember is the priest or whatever he was coming for me at the intermission. Now, that was a setup, wasn't it?"

Gene nodded. "A woman came into the office for an eye examination, just someone off the street. She said she was worried because glaucoma ran in her family and she'd never been tested. You know how we ask if anybody recommended the person? She said no, no one, she wasn't even staying in Winston long, just visiting some relatives. So I tested her for glaucoma—her pressure was fine, normal. She thanked me, and then she asked if I'd ever thought of going to North Carolina for a vacation. I thought it was just chitchat and I said, 'Oh, yes, I've been there. The beaches are excellent.' " Gene stopped. "Did I ever tell you this story?"

"No. Go on—what happened?"

"Well, then she said, 'Laura sent me.' I acted dumb. 'Who?' 'Your sister,' she said. 'I don't know what you mean,' I said. But she told me something that convinced me Laura had sent her. And after that, I just—"

"No, wait, don't go so fast. What did she say about my mother, what was the thing she told you?"

Gene paused in the middle of clearing the table. "My old pet name for Laura. Lala."

"Lala! I never heard that."

"Oh, it's from so far back. Our childhood. You know your mother's ten years younger than I am . . . and when she was born, I was just crazy about her from the first moment. She was such a cute little kid, always dancing and happy, always up on her toes, so I used to tease her, call her Lala the Famous Dancer. . . . Nobody knows that but Laura and me. Yeah, Lala the Famous Dancer. She was like that until she was sixteen, seventeen, then she changed. Very bright girl. She went to college and I remember seeing her once, after she'd met your father. No more dreams of being a dancer. She gave that up entirely, now it was all—the world. Save the world. We're five minutes from midnight, we can't live our lives just for selfish reasons, that sort of thing. She was pregnant then, and I thought, Well, having a baby's going to settle her down." He stopped.

"What got me going on that? Oh, the woman, yes. Well, after she said, 'Your sister, Lala,' I believed her. She had to have that information from Laura, so I agreed to take you down to North Carolina so you could see your parents. I just followed directions. If you asked me now what that woman looked like I couldn't tell you. I probably couldn't have told you the next day. She was just ordinary."

"I never knew any of that."

"Yes, well . . ." Gene wiped his hand across his mouth. "Let me tell you, I was damn nervous when I left you alone in the car at that drive-in. But I'll tell you something else, Pete. I didn't follow their directions to the letter. I got myself in a place where I could watch our car and when that priest came and got you, I went right along. I didn't trust them that much. How did I really know they were bringing you to Laura? I watched you get in that car," he said, leaning across the table to me. "You never knew that, did you? I kept my eye on that car and if they'd tried anything—"

"What would you have done?" My sober uncle lurking in the bushes playing I Spy? It was my first laugh of the morning.

"I don't know," Gene confessed. "I don't know if I could have done anything."

Twenty-three

For days I couldn't walk to school or leave it without
feeling eyes on me, couldn't go into a store or out of
the house without looking around nervously for the
two agents and wondering where they were. In a car?
In an office building? Loitering in the crowded downtown streets? I saw the two of them everywhere.
Even at night, asleep, I wasn't safe from them. Toward the end of the week, as I was walking home
from school, I crossed the boulevard and saw the blue
car with the two agents in the front seat. There it
was—there *they* were—parked boldly in front of a gas
station. Suddenly I was enraged and ran toward
them, shouting. "Why are you watching me? What
do you want? I have nothing to tell you!" I rapped on
the back of the car, rapped on the window.

A man I'd never seen before gave me a frightened
glance. In the passenger seat, the other "agent," a
golden-haired retriever sitting tall, thumped its tail.

"Sorry," I mumbled. "Sorry . . . a mistake."

That sorry incident told me I had to pull myself together. I was OD'ing on paranoia. Sunday morning,
after breakfast, I phoned Cary. "Do you want to do
something today? I do."

"I'm taking Kim to the park."

"Okay, I'll come over."

"If you want to."

Why did she sound so cool? I thought of that rainy afternoon in my room the week before. We'd kissed . . . and kissed . . . then she'd pushed me away, been close to anger. *How about me? How about what I want?* I'd been afraid she'd go away and I'd never see her again, and I'd said, *My parents . . . my parents are in hiding. . . .* I'd been on the verge of saying everything; instead I'd mumbled, chewed up the words.

"I want to see you, Cary."

"Fine." She hung up.

It was a hot, sunny day and the park was crowded. I found Cary pushing Kim on a swing. "Hi!" I was glad to see her.

"Hello." She had on her aloof Princess face.

"Hi, Kimmer."

"Hello, big feet."

Moi?" I glanced at Cary. Not even a hint of a smile. I watched her intently for a few minutes. "What's wrong?"

"Nothing at all."

"Yes, something is. I can tell."

She shrugged. "I'm just wondering why you condescended to come over here this morning. Didn't have anything better to do?"

"Cary, you're not making any sense to me. What are you talking about?"

"Our so-called friendship."

"So-called!"

"Real friends care about each other."

"I care about you. I don't understand."

She glanced at Kim and lowered her voice. "I don't think caring about someone is just a little grabbing and groping—"

That hurt. "Is that all you think I— No, you're wrong."

"You haven't phoned once this week. You haven't stopped in the shop for one moment, even just to say hello.

I fought back. "You could have called me."

"You know how my mother feels about girls calling boys. I want to know just one thing, Pete. Did you stay away because I made it clear I wasn't going to go as far as you wanted?"

"No! No, Cary, that has nothing to do with it."

"Guys don't like it when you say, 'Okay, this far and no farther.' What makes you so different?"

"Maybe I'm not, but I wouldn't not see you because of that. I was just—I've been in a really foul mood. Sort of depressed and . . . you know. I didn't want to dump it on you."

"I want to believe you. I've been thinking the worst things—"

"I should have called, I just—I was so tense and—"

"Did you just get into a blue mood, or what?"

I wanted to hang on to her sympathy. "Something happened. Something bad."

"What was it?"

A line of girls roller-skated by on the walkway, shouting above the clicking of their skates. I stared at them as if they could give me the answer to give Cary. I couldn't tell her about the agents, not without telling her everything. My mind blurred, I felt tired, very tired, and I sat down on a swing.

The chains creaked, a kid yelled, and all at once I was back in a summer afternoon in a park with my mother.

In the middle of the park, there's a stone animal, a rhinoceros. I run up to it, I want to climb on its back, but my mother says children aren't allowed. . . . Anyway, we're playing Hide-and-Seek, it's her turn to hide, and I can't find her. . . . Where ARE you? I yell.

I'm furious, it's not fair for her to hide so long. I yell again, if you don't come back right away, I might get really angry, Laura! Then I hear her laugh, I look all around, and suddenly I find her, lying flat on her belly behind the stone animal. I found you, I win, I win, I shout, and she lets me climb all over her.

Abruptly I hopped off the swing and walked away. I circled the park, waiting for the heat of the memory to cool. When I got back, Cary was sitting on the rim of the sandbox, watching Kim digging. I sat down next to her. "Cary—" I touched her arm and heard myself saying, "The reason I didn't call you has to do with some things I've never told anyone."

I had one cautionary thought—*stop*—and then I went ahead anyway. "It's about my parents. They—they're not dead."

"What?" She stared at me.

"They're not dead. They're in hiding."

"I don't understand. I thought they were dead, you said so. You told me that."

"I know. I had to say it, because of what they did. They bombed a lab, but let me tell you why. It was a protest, a symbolic protest." The words, the images, the ideas, the explanations spurted out, just as I'd imagined and feared, like water flowing irresistibly from an underground spring. Once started, impossible to stem the flow. I couldn't tell what Cary was thinking, I couldn't have stopped if I'd wanted to.

I told her everything. About Laura's and Hal's concern for the earth, and how they'd protested nuclear research and the arms race for years. "They used to go on marches, and demonstrate in front of the White House and the Pentagon, stuff like that. At their graduation from college, when I was just a little kid, they walked out because some general came to speak. They did all sorts of things for years,

141

just kept doing this and that, once they raised a flag on the Statue of Liberty—just to get people to think! It didn't matter what they did, everything kept going on, wars, weapons, the arms race, bombs. They felt things were getting too close to the edge, you know what they say, we're five minutes from midnight. They had to do something that would arouse people, something more than raising banners or symbolically spilling blood."

I knew the phrases by heart. My parents' words. I had grown up with them. But even if I had forgotten them, I had found them again in the library, peppered throughout the newspaper and magazine articles about Laura and Hal. For years these phrases, my parents' words and reasons, had been locked away in my head. Now I was sending them out into the air, into Cary's ear, into the wind. My voice was controlled, neither loud nor soft, but my hands flew apart, I stood up, paced around and sat down again. And all the time, I was also somewhere outside myself, hovering near the swings or perched on the limb of a tree. Pax observing Pete observing Pax spouting off.

"So they bombed a laboratory?"

"Yes. Because it was doing germ warfare research."

"A bomb—but that's so dangerous. Why did they have to do that? Who told them to do it?"

"Nobody told them. They're part of a group, a little group of people . . . Like I told you, all the other stuff wasn't doing any good—"

"Wait, wait!" Cary put up her hand. "Stop. Just stop for a moment. Your parents are wanted people? Like the Ten Most Wanted List? This is not true, is it? It's a sick joke, a put-on." A smile waited at the edge of her mouth.

"Cary," I said as forcefully as possible. "It's the truth. I've told you something no one else knows."

Her mouth quivered, then suddenly she said, "What time is it?" She stood up and looked around. "I'd better take Kim home."

"Cary, wait—"

"What?"

You're right! It's a send-up. Black humor, a cosmic joke. Forget everything I said. "I—why do you have to go now?"

"Kim!" she called. She took the child by the arm, swung her over the edge of the sandbox, and walked away.

"Cary!"

She didn't answer, she didn't turn back.

Twenty-four

"Pete?" Cary said. "Can you talk for a while?"

"I thought you weren't allowed to phone boys."

"I'm not at home. I'm baby-sitting. Anyway, this is special—I really have to talk to you." She started whispering. "It's about your parents, what you told me."

"Look, Cary, I shouldn't have said anything!"

"But you did. And it is the truth, isn't it? I know it is. You're not like other boys, I knew that right away, now I know why. But in the park—I got scared. All I could think was, I can't get mixed up with something like this! I have too many plans and goals! I want to go to college. I want to be *someone*. I don't want to know criminals."

"You want to end this conversation right now?" I said tensely.

"Pete, I'm just trying to tell you what I thought then! I'm ashamed of the way I acted. I know it must have been hard for you to say those things about your parents. You trusted me—it was like you gave me something, a gift, and I threw it away. I've had a lot of things happen to me, and I was always proud that I didn't act like a coward. But Sunday I was afraid, just plain scared."

"So what are you saying, Cary?"

"I'm sorry, that's all, I don't like the way I acted. And I want to go back to the way things were."

"Me, too," I said.

In the Nut Shoppe, I gave Cary a smile. The bell rang, two women came in, then a man, then a bunch of kids. The man couldn't find what he wanted, the kids argued. "Pistachios!" "I hate those little green things." "Frosted walnuts." "Pistachios!" "Sugared almonds." *"Pistachios!"*

Finally they all left. Cary and I held hands for a moment across the counter. "Pete," she said, "I've just been thinking so much about what you told me."

"We don't have to talk about it, Cary." I glanced out the window.

"No, it's not that. I have things I don't tell anyone either. My secrets. Remember the first day, when we went biking? And I told you how my mother was this sick but beautiful person who left me all these beautiful memories?"

"I remember."

"I lied to you. My mother was sick all right, but it wasn't anything like TB or cancer." Her voice was so low I had to lean toward her. "She was a dopehead. Heroin and other stuff too. They took me away from her. They took my sisters away from her. That part was true, and that they put us in different places. And about all my foster parents."

"Cary, you don't have to tell me."

"I want to. This is my truth, Pete. I don't even know when my mother died. I can't remember anyone telling me. Just—one day in second grade, I was sitting at my desk and all of a sudden I knew she was dead. I wanted to cry and I couldn't. I used to pretend she was away getting herself all fixed up and healthy so she could come back for me and my sisters. I don't remember her at all, and I don't want to remember my father."

"Was he that awful?"

"Is. He's still alive."

"I thought you told me your foster parents were going to adopt you for your birthday."

"No problem. My father gave anybody permission to adopt me a long time ago. Only nobody's ever wanted to."

"Why would he do that?"

"He's an alcoholic, and don't tell me it's a sickness. He's a bum. Don't I have a nice family, Pete? Don't I have a wonderful heritage? My father never even came to see me until I was twelve. Then he came to my foster parents' house. He was drunk, dirty . . . he smelled. He wanted money. That's the only reason he came to see me. Pete, I hit him. And another time when I was visiting my sister Amy, he came by. He said he wanted to see Amy's baby."

"Maybe he did."

"Maybe."

"You're hard on him."

"Wouldn't you be? . . . I'm so ashamed of them . . . so ashamed . . ." She started crying.

I didn't know what to do. "Cary, don't . . . it's not that bad." I stroked her arm.

"What's going on here?" Neither of us had heard the door open. A short stout man stood over us.

"Mr. Blutter!"

"Get your stuff together, Cary, you're fired." He pointed at me with a fat hand. "You. Out."

"Sir, can I just say—"

"No. Whatever you two kids were doing, I don't want to hear about it. You go do it in the backseat of a car, not in my store."

My face burned. I couldn't speak. Just when I needed it, my famous maniac impersonation failed me. I waited outside for Cary, kicking myself around for being a coward. When she came out, she looked pretty grim. "I feel terrible that you lost your job, Cary. For whatever it's worth, I blame myself."

"Forget it, Pete."

"Come on, Cary, you want to hit me? I mean it. At least yell at me."

She almost smiled. "Look on the bright side. Mr. Blutter just did me a favor. Now I have no excuse not to look for another job. I'll find something, I always do. I've been working since I was eleven years old. Something always turns up."

"I thought you hated job hunting."

"I do, but so what? Don't you ever do things you hate?"

"Sometimes."

She got that grim look on her face again. "I've done plenty of things I hate." She fell silent.

"You told me Blutter was a beast."

"I was right, wasn't I?"

"Dead on the mark." I stepped over a torn boot lying on the sidewalk.

Cary shuddered. "Every time I see a shoe or a boot lying on the road like that, I think of my father. I saw him once downtown, barefoot, lying in the street on his back, like a dog."

We walked close to each other. "Alcoholism is a disease," I said. "They really have proved that. Anyway, I don't think people are all one way or another. All good or all bad."

"What about Mr. Blutter?"

"Exception to the rule. Your parents had you, you know, so they must have been good underneath."

"Pete, if I turn out to be anyone, it's not going to be any credit to them."

"What do you mean, if—you're someone already."

147

"Am I?" She looked up at me. "Who? Who's that person called Cary Longstreet? Do you know?"

"I think so," I said uncertainly.

"Yes . . . sometimes I think so too. Those are the best times. But other times it seems to me that my whole life is unreal, that I'm just acting, pretending to be someone real, pretending to be that person people call Cary Longstreet. The worst times are when I know I'm not what they think. Then it's like I'm in a play and there are lines I have to learn if I want to stay there—and I do, I do!—but I'm scared so much that I won't learn those lines in time."

Twenty-five

"Did you hear what happened in the game with Tupperville?" Drew said as we left school. The door banged shut behind us. "We were counting on Big Bob and his hitting was off. We barely pulled it out."

"Tough," I said automatically. I was thinking about Cary. Since we'd told each other about our parents, something had changed between us. Not on the surface, but underneath there was something that hadn't been there before: a tension and, at the same time, a new kind of tenderness for each other.

"Drew!" Joanie Casson came running up. She and Drew had been going together again for the past week. "Drew, I've been waiting for you by the office. You were supposed to meet me so we could go down to the museum and check out my stuff. Hi, Pete," she added. Joanie had taken Best of Show in the All-County Student Art Exhibition.

"We didn't say we were going today," Drew said.

"Drew, today is the last day. You promised me. The other day you said definitely you'd go with me."

A blue car pulled up on the road below the slope of the lawn. A man got out and looked around, shading his eyes. It was Frank Miner. I wanted to run, anywhere, any way, any direction, but I kept on walking down the path, straight toward him.

"I told Mom I'd help her out in the store this afternoon," Drew was saying. "I'm sorry, Joanie, the other thing must have slipped my mind—"

"The other *thing?* You know what, Drew? You're a real hypocrite. You want me to come to all your games and jump around and cheer for my hero, but when it comes to me—to something that's important to me—it slips your mind. You keep telling me you love me and then you do things that really hurt." She pulled his ring off her finger. "Here. Take it! I'm not even going to bother throwing it at you this time. And don't think it's just because of the museum. I heard about you being over to Kathy Ransome's house Sunday night. I guess that slipped your mind too."

"We just, we just, we didn't do that much—"

She pushed the ring into his pocket. "Oh, I know, Drew. I've heard it before. We keep having this same conversation, and I'm really bored with it." She walked away.

Drew stood still for a moment, then went after her. And as if that were his cue, Frank Miner hailed me. "Pete." He strolled toward me, his hand out. "Got a minute? This won't take long." He gripped my arm and we walked back to the car.

Jay Beckman was behind the wheel. "Get in, we want to talk to you."

"What do you want? I don't know anything."

"Look, don't give us a hard time."

"I'm not getting in the car."

Beckman's eyes went over me. "You really are a little pain in the—"

"Drop it, Jay," Frank Miner said.

"This kid gets on my nerves, Frank. We've been waiting for him. He knew we were here, he saw us, and he just took his sweet A time. Is this going to be

150

just like the first time? No cooperation? Connors, get in."

"Jay, I'm telling you—leave the boy alone."

The dialogue between the two of them was as neat as a TV show. Good cop, bad cop. I knew it, but I was unable to curb a rush of gratitude toward Frank Miner for defending me. "Pete," he said, "I just want to ask you a few questions." He looked directly into my eyes. "Have you heard from the folks recently?"

"No."

"So it's been a pretty long stretch this time?"

"I don't hear from them."

"No, don't tell me that. They keep in touch. Sure they do. Their own son? What do you do, go out to get their phone calls?"

"They don't call me." I rubbed my lips. Numb.

"Aw, come on. They phone you and they write to you too. They love you, you're their only son."

"I told you," Beckman exclaimed, tapping the steering wheel, "you crap around with this kid and—"

Frank Miner pressed my arm. "Look, Pete, I want to propose something important to you. We want to talk to your people, just speak to them for a while. None of us was born yesterday. I'm not coming around here asking for the impossible. I'm thinking of a phone conversation between me and your pop or your mom. Just a chat, nothing else. What do you think? Can you set it up for us? No strings. You tell them I guarantee that, just a conversation. We've got a proposal to make to them. We've got something to say that should interest them—and you too. You'd like to see your parents home, wouldn't you?"

I tightened my lips and looked past his shoulder.

"Well, think about it," he said. "It sounds like a good deal to me. You can help your parents and us and yourself. Three birds with one stone. After we talk to them, talk some business, I have a hunch they might just decide what the hell, why not come back? It's time."

He lit a cigarette. "No, really, Pete, I'd like to think I had a hand in bringing you and your parents together again. That would give me total satisfaction. Because I like you, I really admire you. I've been thinking about how hard these years must have been for you. No parents. Not using your right name. Nobody knowing about you, who you really are—I mean, that is tough. Really, really tough."

Beckman rolled up the window, then rolled it down. "Are you through crapping around with this kid yet, Frank?"

The other man threw me an apologetic glance. "Okay, okay, we can talk about this next time. Let me give you a ride home, anyway. No, don't shake your head, Pete. It's just a ride, we're not going to kidnap you!" He smiled. "I won't even talk business, okay?"

It was not okay, but, unresistingly, I climbed into the back of the car. Frank Miner got in next to me. "Home, James." He winked conspiratorially at me. We rode almost all the way in silence. Only once, he said, "Is that straight, that you don't get phone calls from your folks?"

"Yes. Turn here."

"I know where your house is," Jay Beckman said.

The next day I met Cary at her school and we walked downtown together. She had some shopping to do. Somehow, we got on the subject of my uncle. "I like your uncle a lot," Cary said. "A whole lot. He's a special person."

"You only met him once, how would you know that?"

152

"I told you, I make up my mind about people really fast."

"Mmm." My mind was on the agents. Why hadn't I told Gene? I felt vague, as if there was a curtain between me and the world. I was here, walking along with Cary, but I wasn't really here, at all.

"Do you think he'll ever get married?"

"What?"

"Your uncle, Pete! Do you think he'll ever get married?"

"I don't know, Cary."

"He's very good-looking for an older man. Doesn't his girlfriend want to get married?"

"I don't know."

"I'd like to get married someday and have children, but it worries me that I might not be a good mother."

"Sure you'd be a good mother," I said automatically.

"What if not loving your kids is hereditary?"

"You mean your mother? She was a sick person."

"A druggie! You're always making things sound nicer."

I blew out my breath, sighed, then heard myself sighing, big dramatic, Gene-type sighs, but I couldn't stop. "Are we fighting, Cary? I don't want to fight with you." Maybe I sounded desperate. I had a feeling of everything falling apart, falling in, caving in. "I don't want to fight with you!"

"Pete." She peered into my face. "Hey, what's the matter?"

"Sorry, I just—"

"I don't want to fight with you either. It's awful when friends fight."

We held hands and it was okay again.

Later, we stopped in to see Martha. "What a neat surprise," Martha said. "This has been a dog of a day, I needed a surprise. Would you believe, not one customer all day?"

"What are all these hats for?" Cary said, examining Martha's wooden tree.

"I'm never sure if it's because I love hats or because it really does make a more interesting picture to put a hat on someone." She put a wide straw hat on Cary's head. "Look in that mirror and you'll see what I mean."

Cary tipped the hat back a little. It had a broad red ribbon hanging down in back.

"Sit down, let me do you just like that," Martha said.

"I don't know," Cary said hesitantly. "How much is it?"

"No, no, nothing." Martha picked up her charcoal stick.

Cary looked scared. "Hey, relax," I said, "it's not like going to the dentist."

"I just never—nobody ever painted me before." She sat down on the stool.

"It's not a painting, hon," Martha said. "Just a little character sketch." She sat down in front of her easel. "I love your forehead . . . yes, stay just like that, that look—that graveness—"

Cary sat with her hands folded in her lap. I stood to one side of Martha while she worked, watching her magic, watching Cary appearing between the charcoal and the paper.

That night, I waited up for Gene to come home from play rehearsal. I must have fallen asleep at the dining room table. I dreamed about the two agents. In the dream, they were themselves, but they were also squat bulldogs, snapping and nipping at my legs. I woke up with a start, groggy, my stomach lurching.

It was almost midnight before Gene came in. "Pete!" His face was flushed. He threw his tattered playscript down on the table. "Listen to this. I'm going to play Lord Fancourt. Harvey Lewis has missed the last three rehearsals."

I pushed the playscript away. "Gene, those two guys showed up again. Yesterday, right after school. I was with Drew—"

"The agents?" My uncle sat down abruptly. "What did they want this time? Drew was with you? That's not so good."

"He didn't notice anything. He's got crazies with his girl friend. They're after me to set up a phone call with Laura or Hal. Gene, I got in their car. What's the matter with me?" I pounded my fist on the table. "They want me to help put my mother and father in jail and I let them drive me home." I jumped up and ran into the kitchen. Gene followed me.

"Take it easy, I'm sure you didn't do anything wrong."

"I got into their bloody car, Gene! If only I could let Laura and Hal know that they've found me." I pulled aside the curtain at the kitchen window. It was a dark cloudy night. "I don't know . . . Maybe I ought to go away."

"What do you mean, away?" Gene said.

"Away. *Away.* Disappear. It might be better for everyone. Laura and Hal, you. I was thinking—next, maybe, they're going to start on you. But if I left . . . I'll go live someplace else, another city . . ."

I stayed at the window, staring out into the darkness, listening to the sounds of my uncle fixing a cup of tea for himself . . . the water pouring into the pot, the clink of spoon against china. I thought about being alone in a strange city . . . walking down long, empty streets . . . looking for someplace to live . . . never seeing Cary again, or Gene, or Martha . . .

"Pete." My uncle gripped my shoulder. "I want you to give me your word that you won't do anything foolish." The warmth of his hand soaked through my skin. "Promise me, Pete."

I nodded. I couldn't speak. The tears were in my throat.

Twenty-six

"I never saw you so dressed up," Cary said as she opened the door.

"Special day." It was her birthday. "You look great." She was all in red—red dress, red shoes, a red band holding back her hair. I held out the box of chocolates I'd bought her. Gift wrapped by the store. "Happy birthday and all that good stuff, Cary."

"Mmm, that smells wonderful. Come on in." I followed her inside. "Feel my hands," she said, "aren't they like ice? Every time I think of what's going to happen today, I start trembling. I hardly slept last night. It's going to happen, it's really going to happen, Pete."

"Cary—what if—listen, you know it's possible they got you something else—"

She smiled. "Uh uh, you're not going to spoil things for me. Pete, I told you, my mother said, 'A really special present.' "

"I know."

"So what else could it be? They know how much I want to be adopted. But when I think that after all these years, I'm going to have a real family . . . When they tell me, I'll cry, I just know I will. I'm talking a lot, aren't I? Do you think they'll just say it, or give me the papers, or what?"

"I don't know, Cary."

"I think it'll be in my birthday card," she said.

We went into the kitchen, where the table was set. When I saw Mr. Yancey in a tie and suit jacket, I was glad I'd listened to Gene and worn a tie too. The whole family was dressed up.

We stood around talking for a few minutes, then Mrs. Yancey said everything was ready and we should all sit down. "Right there, Peter." She put me next to Mr. Yancey. Cary was across from me. The meal started with tomato juice with little wedges of lemon on the lip of the glass, then cream of broccoli soup and hot fluffy rolls. The food was delicious and it kept coming. Cabbage and apple salad, a rib roast, whipped potatoes, buttered green peas and carrots, and more hot rolls.

"Now, before we eat dessert," Mrs. Yancey said, "Cary has to pick a favorite song that we'll all sing. We do this for everyone's birthday, Peter. It's one of our family traditions. Next year, when Cary's eighteen, we'll do the same," she added.

Cary looked at me and I knew what she was thinking. *See! Next year, she said, next year when I'll be their real daughter.*

Cary chose "Bridge over Troubled Waters" for us to sing. The tune is high for me, so I just mouthed the words. The whole time Cary was singing she looked at her foster mother. At the end of the song she hugged Mrs. Yancey. "I love you, Mom, I love you all so much."

"And we love you, honey." Mrs. Yancey's face was flushed almost as bright as Cary's, and I started to think I was all wrong to worry that Cary was setting herself up for a fall. After all, she knew the Yanceys a lot better than I did.

After the cake and ice cream, Mrs. Yancey brought in the presents and gave them to Cary one by one. First a bunch of little presents, knee socks, hairbands, and writing paper. Cary opened everything without rushing, folded the wrapping paper carefully and passed it to her mother. She held up the knee socks and admired them (they were from Kim), replaced her hairband with a new one, and thanked everyone. The chocolates I had brought were passed around the table.

Finally there were just two boxes left, one of them small and flat and one good-sized, plus an envelope. "Mom, save my card for last." Cary glanced at me, smiling. Her next present was an Instamatic camera.

"It's loaded and ready to roll," Mr. Yancey said. "You don't have to do anything but press the trigger."

"This is wonderful!" Cary raised the camera. "Smile, Mom."

Mrs. Yancey took off her glasses. "Cary, I take terrible pictures."

"No, you don't, Mom. You're so pretty."

"Somebody make me smile."

"American cheese," Kim said.

Cary clicked off pictures until the whole roll was shot. Mrs. Yancey handed her the small present. Inside the wrapping was a flat white box and inside that, a coral necklace. "Oh, it's beautiful," Cary said, putting it on. "This has been the best birthday of my life."

"It's not over yet." Mrs. Yancey handed her the envelope. Cary held it to her lips for a moment, then slowly unsealed it and took out the card. On it was a picture of a yellow-haired girl sniffing a large bouquet of red and yellow flowers.

"Read it out loud," Mrs. Yancey said.

"Don't forget to look inside," Mr. Yancey said.

" 'Happy birthday to a dear daughter,' " she read from the cover. She took in a deep breath and opened the card. A hundred-dollar bill fell out on the table. " 'Happy birthday to our dear daughter,' " she read on, " 'and may this remembrance bring you as much joy and happiness as you deserve. Love from Mom and Dad.' "

She turned the card over, then opened it fully. There was nothing else.

Mr. Yancey picked up the money and tucked it into Cary's hand. "Just an extra something we wanted to give you. Because you're a wonderful daughter, a wonderful foster daughter, and we want you to buy yourself something very nice with it."

Cary had gone pale. Carefully, she put the card back into the envelope. "Oh, I will. Yes," she said. "Yes, thank you. Yes . . . something very nice," she repeated.

Twenty-seven

We walked fast, not talking. It was dark, warm, and rainy outside. We sloshed through puddles, turned corners, crossed streets. I kept trying to find something to to say to comfort her. *Tough luck . . . I bet there are lots better parents in the world. . . Don't forget, next year you'll be eighteen and independent.* Dumb. Callous. Better to say nothing. I touched her arm, but she didn't respond. I thought of her smile throughout the meal, and then the way her face went pale when she realized her "special" birthday present was a hundred-dollar bill. What is there to say to someone who's been hurt that much?

Cary walked faster, almost ran. "Cary, wait, wait, let me . . ." Let me what? I didn't know. "Can I—Cary, I want to help you. Tell me what to do."

"You can't do anything." Her face crumpled, she leaned against me. "Pete, they've broken my heart."

We walked again. "My own fault," she said suddenly. "You warned me. And I should have known." She shook her head, hurried as if she were going somewhere, her face lifted and closed.

A door in a house opened, light streamed into the street, and a group of people came running out. "Elizabeth, come on! . . . Oh, no, I forgot the keys! . . . Did you guys take the casserole?"

161

Cary stopped and watched until the whole group of shouting, laughing people got into a car and drove away. The rain came down harder. "Want to go back?" I said. "No. Not yet." She started to cry. I put my arm around her and we walked that way for a while. "Are you still crying?"

She half-laughed. "Can't tell in this weather, can you?"

On the next street, we went into a diner. Everything was green, from the green walls and green curtains to the cracked green vinyl seats. We sat down next to each other in a booth.

The waitress wore a green uniform and handed us a green-covered menu. "Welcome to Green's Diner. You two look like you just came off the ark."

"It's raining pretty hard," I said.

"What'll you have?"

Cary shook her head. "Just a glass of water."

"Milk and apple pie for me."

"A la mode?"

"Okay, make it a double scoop."

"Pete, after all that birthday cake?"

"Whose birthday?" the waitress asked.

"Hers. She's seventeen."

"Congratulations, honey. The best years of your life."

Cary looked up at her. "Thank you, I hope so." She did something with her face and her voice then, smoothed them out, smiled as if her whole world were absolutely perfect.

"You are amazing," I said when the waitress left. "I think you're destined to be another Meryl Streep. I mean it."

"Why?"

"What you just did for the waitress—beautiful performance." For a moment she looked interested. I thought of the many faces of Cary. If she could learn

to bring them out on command . . . "You'd be beautiful on stage."

"You think so?" she said indifferently. Her eyes
faded out again. She pushed aside the curtain and
stared out the dark window.

In the background, the radio was playing love
songs, and in between the disc jockey was giving
time and temperature reports. "It's sixty degrees
and wet tonight, don't forget your umbrellas . . ."

The waitress came around the counter, holding a
tray.

"Green apple pie coming up," I said. "Actually,
what I'm looking forward to is the green milk." I got
a little smile out of Cary on that. The waitress set
down the pie in front of me.

"Want a bite, Cary?" I said.

She fingered the string of coral around her neck.
"Pete, this is real coral. This is not a cheap present."

"I know."

"This and the camera and the money—they went
all out, Pete."

"Sooo . . . give me your heaa-aaart," a singer
wailed, "aaaand I'll give you miii-iiiine!" Then the
DJ was on, excitedly telling us it was twenty-nine before nine and still raining. "What a day, folks! Great
day for the fishes!"

"I wish he would shut up," Cary said. She drank
two glasses of water before I realized she was crying
again. She just sat there, upright, drinking the
water and crying.

I felt so helpless. "Cary—"

She gave that funny little half laugh. "I'm a wa-
terworks today." Then in the next breath, "Pete, do
you love me?" She wound her fingers through mine.
"I don't want you to say it just because—"

"No, I wouldn't."

After another moment, "Did I tell you what they

said to me? They said I was just like a daughter to them. Just like a daughter. That's exactly what they said, Pete."

Our arms touched, and our legs. I ate the pie rapidly, my thoughts drifted, the radio became a hum in my ear. ". . . that dynamite new vocal by The Damsels, who're coming up in the fast lane on the charts—" If only we were in my house now, in my room . . . we could lie on the bed . . .

Kissing and touching . . . touching her wonderful skin . . .

Cary looked at me gravely. Did she know what I'd been thinking? I flushed, then a smile spread across my face, I couldn't stop it. Were my thoughts so bad? I didn't think so. I liked them.

"What's funny?" she said.

"I just like looking at you." It was the truth, but it was also true that as we sat pressed close together, I had had an attack of instant amnesia—forgotten Cary's troubles, and been totally caught up in my fantasy.

When we left the diner, she said, "Do I look like I've been crying?" She pulled up the corners of her mouth. "How's that? They always want to see me smiling."

"Cary, would it be so terrible if they knew they'd hurt you and disappointed you?"

She turned on me fiercely. "Yes! Yes, it would! They don't want to adopt me and that's their business. I'm not begging. I'm not a beggar, Pete!"

Twenty-eight

"Come on in here, Pete." My uncle, white-coated, crooked his finger at me. I followed him into the examination room at the end of the corridor. It was a little room with old equipment that Gene hardly ever used. He closed the door and sat down in the cracked leather chair facing the eye chart. "Yesterday I did a little chore for us. I had a chat with your friends. I laid everything out for them. I made it simple and direct, and I think I got the message across."

I straightened up. "You had a chat with what friends?"

"I talked to the agents, Pete."

"Frank Miner and Jay Beckman?"

My uncle nodded.

"They came here? They came to the office? I was afraid of that."

"No, no, no. Relax. I went to them." Standing up, he straightened a row of toy cars on a shelf. "Look at this, your old Car-a-Rama set. I'd forgotten they were here. I ought to bring them out to the waiting room for kids to—"

"Gene." My voice rose. "You went to them?"

"Right. I went to the district office. I did it for you."

"For me!" My voice went completely out of control.

"Pete, calm down and listen. I did something that had to be done. I talked to them straight. I told them—I told them emphatically—neither you nor I know anything about your parents' whereabouts." Gene spread out his hands. "I put it as plainly as possible, right out on the table. I said, 'Look, if we knew anything, it would be different, but we don't. We—just—don't—know—anything. So, how about you stop wasting your time?' "

"Great. Great going, Gene."

"Pete, you should be thanking me. I called off the dogs. As I pointed out to them, why should they waste their time on a sixteen-year-old boy? They have plenty of other problems—let them go out and find those three guys who robbed Brinks last week. By the way, I should say they were very nice, completely friendly and polite."

"What'd you expect, the KGB?"

"I really thought you'd be glad I went to them."

"Glad? Glad my own uncle is a traitor?"

"You're getting a little rough there. Who'd I betray? What did I do so wrong?"

"Gene! Those are the guys who want to nail Laura and Hal and you went to them and played footsie."

"I did no such thing! I didn't do anything to hurt your parents. You think I'm that sort of person? Turn in my own sister! Look, you know very well I don't agree with her politics—the methods—but that doesn't mean I'm a fink! And I resent your implication, Pete. I resent it deeply."

"Why didn't you ask me before you went to them? It's my life you're messing in."

"Your life has nothing to do with me, I suppose?"

"You suppose damn right!" I shouted. "My life! Leave my life alone!"

Gene looked at me for a long minute. "Fine," he

said softly. "That's just fine. You've made yourself very clear."

"Are you worried about something?" Cary said.

I threw a stone into the underbrush. We were in the little woods behind the post office. "I've been kind of depressed for a few days."

"Well, we're just on a seesaw, aren't we? I got over my depression and now it's your turn. What happened?"

"I had a fight with my uncle." We'd barely talked since that afternoon. Hello, good-bye, pass the sugar—that was about it. Gene's face told his side of the story. I'd hurt his feelings and he was waiting for me to apologize. I told myself he had it bass ackward. Let him apologize to me for trot-trot-trotting off to the agents. But I couldn't forget how I'd shouted at him, *Leave my life alone!*

"A bad fight?"

"Yes. Bad. Very bad."

"Come on, Pete. What could be so bad between the two of you?"

"Plenty. Remember what I told you about the agents trying to get me to talk about my parents?" She nodded. "Well, Gene went to them. He went to them of his own free will. I still can't believe it! It's just an act of, of—" I didn't know what to call it. I pulled my knuckles in frustration, then caught myself. The same thing Gene did when he was agitated.

"He was thinking of you," Cary said. "Trying to help you. And you know something? What if they did find your parents now? Did you ever think they might want to be found? If I'd been hiding for a million years—"

"Eight years, Cary, and if they wanted to be found, they wouldn't need those hound dogs to do it for them!"

"All right, don't get so excited. You sound so mad. I hate it when you yell."

"I'm—sorry." I knuckled my forehead. "I am sorry, Cary, I'm just taking it out on you." I thought about all the times I'd taken my feelings out on Gene, shouted at him, gone into rages when he hadn't done anything to me. Didn't deserve it. Forget it, I told myself, you're starting to feel sorry for him. Forget it!

I squeezed Cary's hand. "Are you mad at me?"

She shook her head.

"You sure? I'm such a jerk sometimes."

"Go ahead, crawl a little, I love it."

"Oh, so that's the way you are!" I flicked my finger at her nose and she punched me in the arm. We wrestled around for a little while . . .

When we settled down again, she said, "Pete. What about the statute of limitations? They can't put people on trial for things they did years ago."

"Cary, no, it's different. That's for things like finding out twenty years later that someone committed a crime. See, then they figure, okay, it's too late to start hauling them into court—except, of course, if it's a capital offense. But as far as my parents are concerned, 'No statute of limitations shall extend to any person fleeing from justice,' quote unquote." I'd looked that one up a long time ago.

She thought about that for a minute. "I guess it makes good sense, or else everybody who committed a crime would run away and wait six or seven years, whatever it is, then come back and be free. But even so, nobody's going to send them to jail for a long time just for bombing a laboratory."

"Where'd you get that idea?"

"If I were on the jury and I knew they did it because they hate war and really had good intentions, just wanted people to listen to them and think about things like germ warfare, how terrible it is—isn't that what you said? Why they did it? If I were on the jury, I'd take that into consideration. And another thing I'd take into consideration is that being in hiding for so many years is probably almost like jail, anyway. Don't you think so? It's really like being punished by yourself, isn't it?"

I looked at her for a moment.

"Maybe."

"It is," she said insistently. "Any normal person on a jury would think so. Hiding—" As if the word itself were something foul, she drew herself together, into herself, almost shuddered.

And I thought how, in a way, it wasn't only my parents who were in hiding. Cary and I were hiding too. I knew about me. And the more I knew about her, the more I knew that what she showed the world was just what she wanted to show the world. Or maybe just what she wasn't afraid to show the world.

I felt close to her and took her hand. It was warm, or maybe mine was cold. "You don't know the whole thing about my parents, Cary. I didn't tell you everything." She turned her face up to mine, and I went on doggedly, saying what I'd avoided saying or thinking for so long. "If my parents come back — Listen, two people died in that bomb blast."

"Died?"

"They weren't supposed to be there, nobody was supposed to be there in the lab, nobody."

"Pete—"

"And my name's Pax Connors, not Pete Greenwood. Pax Martin Gandhi Connors. And now you really know everything about me."

From the Manila Envelope

Services Held for Jameson, Udall, Killed in Lab Bombing

Ralph S. Jameson, professor of molecular biology at Beecham University, and Kin Udall, a graduate student who had been working with Dr. Jameson, were buried today by their families in Woodcrest Cemetery on South Point Road. Although Ms. Udall's family resides in Bethesda, Maryland, they acceded to the request of the Jameson family that she be laid to rest near Dr. Jameson, with whom she had worked over the past year as a graduate assistant.

"Ralph was terribly fond of Kin," Nora Jameson, Dr. Jameson's widow, said. "Ralph had several graduate students working with him, but he and Kin had worked together especially closely. He thought highly of Kin's potential. Kin was a very talented young woman. She had a great future ahead of her. Ralph brought her and her boyfriend home for dinner several times and all of us were fond of her. She was just a very, very, nice, bright young woman."

Dr. Jameson and Ms. Udall were both killed in the bombing of Femmer Laboratory Thursday night. Responsibility for the bombing has been claimed by an organization known as Air, Water, Earth.

Dr. Jameson's son, Norris Jameson, said, "My dad loved his country. These people who did this thing are killers. They are without conscience or heart. When the police catch them, I will sit in the courtroom and cheer when they're sentenced to death."

Dr. Jameson leaves his widow, Nora Delblanco Jameson, two sons, Ralph S. Jameson, Jr. of Portland, Oregon, and Norris Jameson of Red Bluff, California, and one sister, Mrs. Farley Allen of Santa Monica, California.

Ms. Udall leaves a sister, Monica Udall, and her mother, Harriet Udall, both of Bethesda, Maryland.

Mrs. Udall is in poor health and did not attend the funeral.

There have been unconfirmed reports that research in aspects of germ warfare, possibly involving genetics, has been under way in Femmer Lab. When contacted, university officials refused to comment.

Twenty-nine

Saturday was the opening night of *Charley's Aunt.*
Gene came home early from the office. I was watching TV. "So . . . ," I said, feeling that I had to say
something. "Tonight's the big night."

Gene managed a wan smile. "It sure is. I'm going
to take a nap. If I'm not up by five-thirty, will you
wake me?"

"Okay." Our fight hadn't been resolved and we
were still stiff with each other. It seemed as if we
were each waiting for the other to make the first
move, apologize or admit he was wrong—whatever.

Later, around six o'clock, after Gene had already
left for the theater, I went upstairs to shower and
change. I was supposed to pick Cary up at seven.
"I'm doing this for you, Gene," I said, shining my
shoes. I put on a clean shirt, picked out one of Gene's
ties, and found a matching pair of socks in his bureau.

Downstairs, I flipped on the TV. I was still struggling with the tie, when the phone rang. It was Mrs.
Yancey.

"Peter? I'm really sorry to tell you this, but Cary
won't be able to go to the play tonight."

"I was just on my way out for her—"

"She woke up sick this morning, some kind of flu. I

kept her in bed all day. Do you want to speak to her? Just for a few minutes, though."

Cary got on the phone. "Isn't this the worst, Pete?" Her voice was hoarse. "I feel just miserable about missing out."

"I'm going to miss you," I said. I walked the phone into the dining room and sat down on the steps and idly watched what was on the boob tube.

"I don't think I'd even last the bus ride. You're going to go, aren't you?"

"I have to, Cary. This is the big enchilada— opening night. You should have seen my uncle. Nervous doesn't half cover it."

"Will you tell him how bad I feel? I wanted to be there so much."

"He'll be sorry, too." I glanced at the TV. On the screen a long-haired woman in a skirt and blouse, her arm linked with that of a man holding a briefcase, hurried up a flight of stone steps. Reporters chased after them, holding out microphones and yelling questions.

"Call me tomorrow and tell me all about it," Cary said.

"Yes . . . sure . . ." I stared at the TV. The barking cries of the reporters, the bland voice-over of the newscaster, and Cary's hoarse coughing all mingled in my head.

" 'Bye!"

" 'Bye."

I dropped the phone. I'd barely seen the woman on the screen, and yet I knew who she was. Something about the angle of her shoulders, some buried memory of her just that way . . . back straight, legs striding purposefully up stairs, away from me, toward a massive columned building . . .

The picture on the television changed and the anchorman appeared, serious, sincere, his hair blow-dried into place, his lapels neither larger nor smaller than lapels ought to be. Behind him, boxed high on another screen, was frozen the moment when the man holding the woman's arm had thrown out his hand to brush away the reporters.

I stood there, transfixed, stunned, trembling. It was Laura. My mother. I hadn't heard her name. I hadn't seen her face, but I knew beyond any doubt. And some awful grief, something ancient and nameless, rolled over me.

Thirty

A woman in a drooping skirt and brilliant yellow leotard top pulled the big wooden door of the playhouse shut. "No hurry," she said. "It's just getting a bit chilly in there. You've got plenty of time."

I walked up the worn steps toward the stone Star of David carved above the door. I had seen that six-pointed stone star innumerable times, but now it struck me as forcefully as a blow to the heart. I had never thought of myself as Jewish, no more than I thought of myself as Irish. I had never thought of my mother as Jewish. My mother's parents, yes, the grandparents I'd never known, but me—I wasn't anything in that way.

People streamed around me, entering the theater, murmuring, laughing. I looked up at the stone star. *Oh, please . . . oh, please . . .* What I was pleading for I didn't know, yet it seemed to me the closest to real prayer I'd ever come. *Oh, please . . . oh, please . . .*

Inside, I handed over my ticket. A slip of paper had been inserted in the playbill, stating that Gene would play Lord Fancourt and Howard Faulk would play Brassett.

"Excuse me." A tall thin girl, her face and arms as spotted as a leopard's, pushed past me. "Do you think they'll start on time? My friend is late."

What if I stood up, clapped my hands, and yelled, *Listen, everybody. Pay attention. My mother is back.*

"I've never seen this theater company before. Are they good?"

I made an effort to act normal. "My uncle's in the play."

"Oh, I see." She smiled at me and, for some reason, I felt almost crazily grateful. Then Martha came and sat down next to me. Her hair flopped around her shoulders. She wore a purple dress printed with green parrots. "Hi, sweetie. Where's Cary? Are you nervous? I am! I'm probably more nervous than Gene." I said something, stared at the mad-looking parrot on her shoulder.

My mother is back. Back. Returned. The sojourner from strange lands, from the underground, from the land beneath the land, from somewhere that was no-where, that was yet somewhere. And how had she done it? Had she burst through the earth, red hair flying, arms outstretched? Wonder Woman! But when I had seen her, she had only been hastily but sedately walking up stone steps to a courthouse. A man, not my father, had held her arm and fended off the reporters. A scene from a movie to be called *Courthouse,* or *Justice.* But real. A documentary. A movie about real people, starring my real mother, who had returned to the real world, suddenly changing all the rules of the game I had played for eight years. The game of Pete-not-Pax.

The lights dimmed, the curtains drew back. Something was happening onstage. Voices chattered, actors came and went. Gene made his entrance and Martha nudged me.

"I've been indiscreet," Lord Spettigue informed the audience in a nasal aside. "Oh, I am sorry, very, very sorry," he said obsequiously to Donna Lucia, the rich widow. Donna Lucia, actually young Lord

Fancourt disguised in a long skirt and bonnet, actually my uncle, flapped "her" fan vigorously, whisking it against Lord Spettigue's pompous face.

Martha leaned toward me, whispering. "Gene looks much better than I expected. Don't tell him, but I was sort of worried. He's not exactly your typical English college boy. But I think he's really carrying it off, don't you?"

Had I really seen my mother? The moment on the TV screen passed behind my eyes, like a dream: something half remembered, shadowy, doubtful. A woman went up a flight of steps. A man held the woman's arm. The steps led to a courthouse. A woman holding a man's arm went up a flight of steps. Yes, a dream. Or a memory. Or a wish. I must have wished that scene into being!

But there was something wrong with my wish picture . . . something—someone—missing. Where, for instance, was my father? Where was Hal Connors in that picture? Was he walking up another flight of stairs in the grip of another lawyer?

During the intermission, standing in the lobby, I heard someone say my name, my real name. *Pax.* I turned my head sharply. But no one was speaking to me, no one was even looking at me. Later as the play ended and the actors took their bows, it happened a second time. *Pax.* Was it my mother, calling me over the miles? Everyone stood up, but I sat there, waiting to hear my name again.

"Pete." Martha hauled me to my feet. "I told Gene we'd meet him at the cast party."

The party was held in Regina's, a restaurant around the corner from the playhouse. People milled around the long tables, eating and drinking. A cloud of smoke hung over the room.

"I think it went wonderfully, don't you?"

". . . almost forgot my lines in act three, then they came to me as from above."

"Lover! You were fabulous! How was I?"

Gene appeared and put his arms around me and Martha. "So what do you think, my people? How'd we do? Was all the work worth it? I don't know if I'm up or down. I had the most god-awful case of stage fright before I went on. Panic, panic. Halfway through the first scene, it left me, just like that." He snapped his fingers.

"You're up," Martha said. "Definitely up."

"I'll really be up if we get a good review. See that little guy over there, the one with the wild mustache? Donald Friedman. He writes the reviews for the *New Winston Times*. If he likes us, we'll have full houses. If not—" Gene drew his hand across his throat.

I left early. At home I went straight to my room, took the manila envelope from its hiding place and emptied the contents on my bed. There were the letters from my parents. There were the articles and the pictures I had collected about them. It was their lives and, by extension, my life. I picked up the article with the picture of my parents on their graduation day: my father holding the small Pax on his shoulders, my mother gesturing to the reporter, both of them wearing black graduation robes. The tassel from my mother's mortarboard fell over her face, giving her a rakish look.

She had returned to this world and never let me know that she was coming. She must have made plans, talked to people, written letters, made phone calls. That lawyer wasn't there by accident. But no phone calls to me. No letters. No messages. I had had to watch the evening news to find out my news. "Laura," I yelled. "Laura! Laura! Laura!" I pounded the walls like a madman, crying and cursing. My eye

178

fell on the letters. I crumpled and tore them. The phone rang. I tore Laura's picture and threw it to the floor. The phone rang again. "Shut up, shut up." I tore up everything, all the letters, all the articles, tore them into smaller and smaller pieces.

Thirty-one

In the morning, the phone ringing downstairs got me out of bed. "Pete, you sound half asleep," Martha said.

"I am," I said, but I'd been up for hours, thinking about my mother . . . trying to think about her. All these years, eight years, half my life, I had been without her. There had been the visits, of course— yes, the visits—and what did they mean? They had been so brief, so intense, so frightening and awful. After each visit, I had always been depressed for days, given Gene a rough time. I remembered how, right after seeing Laura and Hal in North Carolina at the drive-in movie, I had barely spoken for a week, sleepwalked through the days.

"Is Gene awake yet?" Martha said.

"No."

"Well, let him sleep. I'm coming over with croissants, put on the coffee. Maybe the smell will rouse our star. Did you see the review?"

"No."

"Read it. It's neat. A few little crits, but that's to be expected. Gene, and everybody, should be happy, I'd say. See you in a while."

I took in the newspaper, spread it out on the kitchen table. The article about my mother was on the second page. FUGITIVE SURRENDERS TO FEDS. There was a smudged picture of her next to the article.

I had thought I was calm, but I couldn't bring myself to read the article. I stared at the photo for a long time. Was that really Laura? How could I know? How could I be sure? I had read a story in the paper about two sisters who had been reunited after fifty years. "I would have known her anywhere," the older sister said. Wasn't that what a son should be able to say about his mother? *I'd know you anywhere* . . . But would I? What if I saw Laura in a crowd of strangers? What if there were two red-haired women in that crowd? What if two women came up to me and each one said, *"I'm* your mother, come with me." Would I know which one to choose?

Last night, seeing Laura on the TV, I had known who she was. But this morning, I was uncertain of everything. I thought of those moments in motels and drive-in movies when I had seen her, I thought of the newspaper pictures I had studied so often. I thought of my own memories. And all of it seemed to add up to nothing concrete, nothing solid or real. Laura . . . who was she? What was she? Laura, the invincible . . . the certain . . . Laura, the Wonder Woman . . . Laura, the miracle worker, out to save the world.

To save the world . . . to save the world . . . "Oh, yeah!" I said it out loud. "Oh, yeah!" It came out hard, clenched, mean between my teeth. *Save the world forget your son drop a bomb two people dead who cares go away run hide I'll help being good never cry never deny good boy I'm good my mother's son my father's boy mature grown-up responsible stay with Uncle Gene never be mean do my share we all care save the world save the world save the world . . .*

I spun around the room, pounding the floor, pounding the counters, slamming my fist into the fridge, against the stove. Oh yeah oh yeah oh yeah, breathing hard, something in the chest, something in the throat, gritty lump, lump of anger, nowhere to go, just sitting there, lumpy lumpy lumpy . . .

I opened the back door, stuck my head out, breathed in the cool wet morning air. Faint city hum, the ailanthus in bloom, a jet streak like a message in the sky.

I sat down at the kitchen table. Look at the picture again, read the article, you can handle it. Picture first. A head shot, Laura grimacing, turning away from the photographer. Was it she? Laura? My mother? Yes . . . no . . . yes . . . The smudged photograph was like a trick picture where the image appears and disappears and appears again.

The article described her as "weary" and "soft-spoken."

"In a soft voice, Connors directed all questions, including those about her husband, Hal Connors, also wanted on the same charges, to her lawyer, Porter G. Danbury, who was at her side throughout. However, she did read a brief prepared statement. 'I have returned to face the charges against me. Long ago, I dedicated my life to working for a peaceful, non-violent world. Yet, through my actions, two people died. With the passing of time, it has become harder, not easier, for me to live with this knowledge. I don't think justice can ever truly be served in this situation, nothing will bring them back, but nevertheless I feel compelled to pay whatever the penalty will be. Thank you.' Connors was remanded before Federal Judge Ivan B. Percolo and then taken to the Women's Correctional Institute on Ellis Island in New York City."

I dropped the newspaper. So that was why she had

come back. And why now? And why not last year? And why not the year before? Laura, who are you?

All of a sudden I was ravenous. I pawed through the cupboards and refrigerator, stuffing my mouth with cold hot dogs, a half-chewed apple, soggy rolls that smelled mousy. I was a garbage can, opening my mouth, shoving in all the stale, spoiled, rotting food. Crumbs and bits of food spattered over the floor. Impossible to tell if my stomach ached from hunger, panic, rage, or food poisoning.

The phone rang. *Laura.*

From upstairs, Gene called, "You getting that, Pete?"

I picked up the receiver, but fumbled it and cut the connection.

The ringing began again. "What's going on?" Gene appeared in his striped shortie pajamas.

"It's probably a wrong number."

"Maybe it's Broadway calling me." He picked up the receiver. "Hello? . . . Oh, yes, I missed you . . . Well, now that's too bad . . . You'll have to come when you're—" He beckoned me. "Sure, he's right here, Cary." He sat down at the table and thumbed through the newspaper, going past the second page without a glance.

"Hello," I said to Cary, and then, remembering, "how are you feeling?"

"Not too good. My throat is killing me."

Gene whistled for my attention and held up the newspaper so I could read the headline. STRONG PRODUCTION OF OLD FAVORITE PLEASES AUDIENCE. He put his thumb and forefinger together.

"Martha called—she told me."

"What?" Cary said.

"I was talking to Gene. His play got a good review."

"Oh, wonderful, tell your uncle I'm happy for him."

"I'll do that. Listen, I'll talk to you later, okay?" I hung up. "Gene—she came out."

He plugged in the coffeepot. "Out? Out where? Who where?"

I turned to the second page. "Read that."

He was still smiling as he bent over the paper.

Just then, Martha came in with the croissants and several more copies of the paper. "Ta ta! How about that review?" she said, kissing Gene. He made an odd choked sound.

"I saw it on TV last night," I said. Gene glanced at Martha, warning me. "It doesn't matter anymore, Gene. The whole world's going to know."

"Know what?"

"When did you see it on TV?" Gene asked.

"The six-thirty news."

Martha looked from one of us to the other. "What's going on?"

"It's—just—" Gene picked up the coffeepot, then put it down. "My God, this changes everything, doesn't it?"

"If one of you doesn't tell me right now—"

"It's my mother. She's come back."

"Very funny," Martha said coldly. "I do not think jokes about the dead are in good taste."

"Tell her," I said to Gene.

"Where do I start? How— Pete, you—"

"No," I said. "You do it." I walked out.

Thirty-two

My dear, dear, dearest son,

I don't know where to start this letter. I have come back. Do you know that already? And I want to see you. I want to see you! I'm in prison, but I want you to come here anyway. I don't want to wait to see you. I am overflowing with feelings, emotions. I am shaking as I write this because I know that I can see you again soon, very soon, and that this time it won't be for five minutes or fifty minutes, and that when "our hour" is over with, you won't disappear for another two years. I don't think you can possibly imagine what this means to me. To see you once again almost at will—of course, there will still be restrictions because I'm in prison, but they'll seem such tiny restrictions compared to what we've known!

I tell myself to go slowly, that we have years to recover, years ahead of us too, but I am so impatient, I want so much to see you, to hold you—then I remind myself that you are no longer my little eight- or ten-year-old son, that you are sixteen, nearly a man—and I'm frightened. I tell you truthfully, I am frightened—I will always love you, how could I do otherwise, but how do you feel about me? I couldn't think of this, not in real terms, when I was away, it was too dangerous, too hard, too threatening. But now, along with so much else, I am facing this question. I take a deep breath and write—because I am determined that we will be honest with each other. Do you resent me? Do you hate me? No, I know you don't. You couldn't, you mustn't! But I must face that you are someone I don't know anymore, that you have a life I know nothing about. I want us to be together again, to be mother and son, to be a family—oh, I know it can't be wholly that, because I have a trial to face, a prison sentence. Yet we could be near each other through this. We could have some life of our own.

I love you, my son. And your uncle, my brother—what a blessing he has been to me all these years. I knew, at the very least, you were cared for and loved by someone who was family.

I'll try to write a more coherent letter next time. I'm very tired. Please write to me. I am starved for news of you.

All love,
Mom

P.S. Please give the enclosed to your uncle.

My dear good brother,

By now, from the newspapers and TV you must be aware that I've returned and the immediate consequences of that return. I am now in the Women's Correctional Institute, facing indictments on several serious charges. My lawyer is working to have me released on bail, but I am not too hopeful of that outcome.

Nor do I think I will esc—get away without a prison sentence. I started to write "escape without a prison sentence." So it seems my mental set is still one of flight and hiding. I don't think it will be easy to shake off some of the effects of the last eight years. To live every day looking over your shoulder, wondering if the steps coming up the stairs are for you, always needing to be alert and sometimes—so often!—so tired of it all—but I don't want to get started on that now.

Let me just say this. I believe I will have to serve a prison term for what I did, and, indeed, in some sense *I want to.* I am not a masochist, but this is why I returned. To do penance, to pay the price society sets, however paltry it may seem compared to the loss of lives for which I am responsible. And I do take responsibility, although I was part of a group and carried out a group decision. And do you wonder, Gene, why I return now? Why come back now, at this time, at this particular juncture? I can only say that to have arrived here, at this moment in my life, has been a process. I have been on the way to this moment for a long time. I suppose everything in life is a process, but that is cold comfort when I think back over the past eight years.

I have never forgotten the two lives that were sacrificed. I thought I would come to terms with those deaths, but as time passed, it has come to seem to me not a lesser, but a greater offense against nature and life. Life must be preserved. That was where I started years ago, in a revulsion against war and killing. And of all the things that have happened to me over the years, that is the one steady point of light. Yet I was the instrument, the cause, of the loss of life.

I refused at first to accept this. I couldn't. I told myself, "You didn't kill. You didn't know. It was an accident—something unforeseen." Time after time, I buried the part of me that did not accept these excuses. That is what I have come to—they were, are, excuses. Each one of us must account for ourselves in this life and to our fellow human beings, or else life has no meaning. And that I do not believe and cannot believe and never will believe. Did you see the movie about Mahatma Gandhi? I wept through the whole thing. I couldn't stop crying, and that was when I knew I couldn't go on any longer.

Well, I must stop now. It's time for exercise. Dear Gene, there will never be words with which I can thank you for what you did.

Love,
Laura

My dear,

A prison is no place to be private, to have one's own thoughts. But I don't mind too much. I find myself getting along with the women in here, finding a great deal in common. Isn't that strange? I'm a political, and most of them are in here for quite other reasons. Yet nearly all of us have children, and that links us. We don't talk much about why we're here, instead we talk about our children and our childhoods.

My son, I miss you. Three years, three long years,

since we've even seen each other. How much you must have changed. I'm longing and longing to see you again, to kiss you, to look at you, to listen to you, to get to know you. In some ways, it's harder for me to wait patiently than it ever has been before.

Now I come to something very difficult that I must tell you. I've been putting it off, but that's unfair. I know you realize by now that Hal did not come back with me. I feel sad to tell you this, but your father and I are no longer together. We have agreed to disagree, not only in our political frame of reference, but personally. I still have and always will have the greatest affection and respect for Hal, but the fact is, we haven't lived together for two years. There are no words that will tell you how sorry I am to have to give you the news this way. My only consolation is that I have faith that you are old enough, mature enough, and stable enough to take it in stride.

For the past eight years, we've lived, as you might imagine, under deeply stressful conditions, and they took their toll. Initially, we decided to separate in order to cut down the chances of our being found. But we discovered that more and more, we were going our separate ways. Disagreements appeared on a number of fronts. I can't tell you everything in this letter, although I want to tell you as much as possible. The important thing is, first, I developed serious doubts about the wisdom of continuing the life of hiding, hit-and-run actions, etc. Doubt is pernicious, it worms its way into one's mind and is, quite literally, poison to someone in my situation. I became ineffective—well, your father disagreed, but at least in my own mind that was the verdict.

And, then, my obsession (your father's word) with being "punished" (as he said; I say, "with taking responsibility") for the lives lost—that, especially, came more and more between us. We do not see eye to eye on this, obviously. So, after much discussion and not a little heartbreak, we realized that our marriage had run its course.

And at last, against Hal's will, I made my decision to return. Strangely, in prison, I am now experiencing a kind of peace I have not had for eight years.

We'll talk more about all these things. We have kind

good friends here, who have offered to take you in, to give you a home with them so we can be near each other. Will you come?

I enclose the address of our friends. They have a room for you and you can go to them without hesitation.

All my love,
Laura

Dear Pax,

Today I was remembering when you were born, with what joy and belief Hal and I named you. Your special name—to honor Martin Luther King and Mahatma Gandhi, those two giants among men, both believers in nonviolence. And for the first time in I don't know how long, I thought of Gandhi's belief in ahimsa—nonharming of others. It was one of the profoundest beliefs of his life.

That was what Hal and I both thought and believed would be our way, too. And we never did hurt anyone—not till that night, and now I ask myself, "How did we do that, how could we have been so sure no harm would result?" But we were sure, sure with the sureness of those who believe in a way that blinds them to reality. The belief makes the reality. Do you understand? I myself am just beginning to understand this, to realize that in the beginning passion motivated me, a longing to do something good for and in the world, and that gradually, through a process I can hardly trace, passion was replaced with a mindset—this is Right, that is Wrong—everything known before the event. Therefore, it was Right to do what we did and no Wrong could come of it, since Wrong was always coming from the Others. Yes, in writing this, I see that what had been fluid and flowing in me became hard and frozen, as a river becomes ice in winter.

And this is why we did what we did, why we went away from the consequences, away from you. It seemed imperative. Our work, we said. Our work has to go on. After all, we said, had these people not been doing the bloody work of the generals, work that could lead to the destruction of thousands, no millions, of lives, had they not been dipping their hands into the blood of innocents, they wouldn't have died.

Not good enough. Not anymore. I am so sad. I have been sad for a long time.

I'll write again. Still no word from you.

Love,
Mom

Thirty-three

"What do you kids want today?" the man behind the counter said. He gave Cary a big smile. It was a hot day, but cool and white inside the ice cream shop. I stared at the garish red, purple, and pink posters of ice cream sundaes and sodas over the counter. Unreal. Everything seemed unreal to me, even being with Cary.

"I really want to go to your uncle's play," Cary said as we sat down in a booth with our ice cream.

The play! I almost smiled. It was so far away from me. "You've got time, it's running for another two weeks."

"Let's go together. You wouldn't mind seeing it again, would you?"

"I don't know, Cary, I'm not sure what my plans are . . ."

"What do you mean?"

"My mother—did you see the article?"

She nodded. "After you told me about it, I got the newspaper and read it. It said she was in prison."

"She is. Did you tell your parents anything about it?"

"No, Pete, are you kidding? They wouldn't—you know, if they knew, they wouldn't even want me to talk to you on the phone."

"And what about you—how do you feel?"

"Well . . . it's not a total shock."

"But it is a shock, right? That my mother's in prison." It wasn't easy to say that, but if I couldn't say it to Cary—

"It's just— When you told me about her and your father, Pete, it was more like—a story. Do you know what I mean?" She leaned toward me. "I don't mean I didn't believe you. It just wasn't—it wasn't entirely real to me. I met your uncle and—to tell the truth, I sort of let the whole thing about your parents go out of my mind."

I knew what she meant. She'd told me all that stuff about her foster homes, but what was vivid and real to me was the Yancey family. I'd forgotten most of the details of her foster homes.

"My mother wants me to come live near her. She's got it all arranged, these friends of hers in the city—"

"New York City? That's a long way away." Cary looked remote, brooding.

A silence fell. We were right next to each other, but very far apart. I didn't have the energy even to try to break through to Cary. I sat there, tapping the spoon against the dish, trying to think clearly about Laura's letters, but I didn't have the energy for that either. What was the matter with me? Why wasn't I clicking my heels and shouting hallelujah? Mother and son reunion coming up just over the horizon. From now on, no more secrets, the clouds lifted, the sun-son shining forever. Only one little flaw: she was in prison (although not forever). No, two little flaws: no father in the rosy dawn. Laura and Hal were no longer Laura-and-Hal. They were Laura. And Hal. I got the feeling Laura told me about her and Hal, let out a big sigh of relief, and figured I'd be, well, not glad, but *understanding*. I wasn't understanding. I didn't understand, I didn't *want* to understand.

Goddamn it! First I had no mother and no father, and now I had a mother in jail and still no father.

I scraped up the last of the ice cream. "If I do go, Cary, I'll come to see you every weekend."

"No you won't!" She shrugged and said flatly, "People don't come back."

"My mother did. Eight years . . . and she came back."

"Is that how long I'm going to have to wait to see you again, Pete?"

"It was just an example."

"You're going there to her, aren't you? I know you are."

"I don't even know it myself yet."

"Well, what are you waiting for? You'll go. To see your mother? You will." She flung out her arm as if she wanted to hit me, then said very clearly, "Don't think your parents are any better than mine, Pete."

"What? . . . I don't—"

"Oh, come on! You think they're superior. Superior moral beings! I've heard you talk about them— 'Everything they've ever done, Cary, is for their principles, not for selfish reasons.' "

Was that how I sounded—pompous and self-important? "Cary, just because I said those things—"

The man behind the counter looked over at us. "Everything okay, kids?"

"Wonderful," I said.

Cary put her face close to mine. "My parents were pretty cruddy, but don't forget—your mother killed two people."

My hand ached, I wanted so much to slap her.

I pushed my dish aside. "Well, this is a real nice time we're having. It's so nice I guess I'll go home." I threw a couple of dollars down on the table and walked out.

Cary's words came with me. *Your mother killed two people.* Laura had said it in her letters too, but in other words. . . . *two lives sacrificed . . . grief for the loss of life . . .* Cary had not been so polite.

Your mother killed two people. Killed, as in murdered. The knowledge had always been there in the back of my mind, but I had thrown up a wall against it, built the wall high, pretended that behind it there was nothing, except perhaps other words. The wall had been shaky for a long time, but now it was tumbling, bricks and boards battered me. Two real people with real names and real bodies and real families were dead. Had been dead for eight years. Laura hadn't shot them, strangled them, stabbed them. She hadn't wanted to hurt them . . . but they were still dead. Bodies exploded, an arm flew across the room, a leg lay twisted under a table, fingers and toes, bloody little body flowers, were scattered in the rubble. My mother killed two people.

"Pete . . ." Cary ran up to me.

I stared at her. *You're right, Cary, my parents are no better than your parents. Worse, actually. Your parents never hurt anybody but themselves—and you.*

"Pete, I don't know why I said that, it just—it just came out." She pulled at the string of coral around her neck.

We crossed the street. I wondered who else thought about the bodies. Gene? Cary? Martha?

"Pete, I'm not telling the truth. I'm jealous. I'm jealous of you. Even though your mother's in jail, she's *here,* and you can go to her. Anytime you want to, you can go to her."

"Oh, yes—and what if I said I was jealous of you, Cary?"

"Don't try to make me feel better, Pete. I said a

194

mean thing." She put her hand on my arm. "Are we still friends?"

"Yes, sure."

"Do you mean it?"

I looked at her, for the first time that afternoon really looked at her. "I mean it." I leaned my forehead against hers. "Cary, I mean it, I mean it."

"I never realized how much of a Midwest hick I am," Martha said, "until Gene told me about all this stuff with your parents, Pete. I mean, I just couldn't believe it. Couldn't take it in. It was like SMERSH or James Bond or something. Pure fiction."

"Didn't you ever think that my parents both being dead was sort of phony?"

"No. Why? No, I believed it. I just— Once I remember thinking it was a little strange you didn't have any pictures of your parents, but then I thought, Well, it hurts too much. Actually, I still find it hard to believe."

"Yes. Right." I remembered the morning in the park when I'd told Cary. She'd been no more prepared than Martha, but after the first doubts, she had believed it as completely as if she could relate to the peculiar parts of my life better than the normal parts. And she didn't beat the subject to death the way Martha did. Martha couldn't leave it alone.

"Your mother just left you? . . . A little kid of eight? . . . She put a bomb in that lab . . . but she must have known somebody could get hurt . . ." Every time, my stomach churned. She kept calling to chew it over. Finally, I blew.

We were in the living room waiting for Gene, waiting to go out to supper before the play. Martha started in. "But didn't your mother think—"

"Can it! You've asked me the same asinine questions a thousand times."

I saw the hurt, the surprise come over her. My temper tantrums had been reserved for Gene. Not Martha, especially not Martha.

They went out to eat without me. The next day I went by her place and apologized. She hugged me. "No, Pete, it's my fault. You've got every right to be sensitive about— Look, *I'm* sorry."

So we left it at that. We were friends again, but I couldn't help wondering how much of my life would be spent answering those very same questions.

"So Laura wants you to pick up and go?" Gene snapped his fingers. "Just like that? What about school? Don't you think you should finish the term?"

I crunched a chicken wing between my teeth. "Maybe."

"Just one more month and then exams."

"Uh huh."

"Poor judgment to transfer to another school now."

"Maybe." I wiped my fingers down the sides of my jeans.

"Maybe, maybe! Come on, Pete, you can do better than that." Gene's eyes bulged. There was a sheen over his face, a greenish cast. "And I'd appreciate it if you didn't eat in the living room without a tray. I've told you that before."

I grabbed my plate. "It's lousy chicken anyway. Undercooked. I think I'll have the rest of the roast beef."

"I ate it for lunch."

"Thanks," I said bitterly. I slumped back against the couch.

"So what are you going to do?" my uncle said. "I'd like to know."

"I haven't made up my mind yet." Gene sighed, big irritated sigh. So instead of irritating my uncle, why wasn't I upstairs packing my things and writing letters?

First a letter to my mother.

Dear Laura, or should I call you Mom?

I noticed you signed two of your letters that way, but to be totally honest (as you said) I think of you as Laura. And what comes to mind is, Who is Laura? That's an old song, you know, I heard it on a golden oldie program one night, Laura, Laura, who is Laura—something like that. I got sort of upset and flipped the radio off, so I might not have heard it just right. But you get the idea. Laura, Laura, who is Laura . . . Dear Laura, dear Mom, dear Mother, I want to come to you—I think. Total honesty, right? Something's holding me back. Don't know what it is. Do you? If so, let me in on the secret. Love, Pete. Pardon me, Love, Pax.

Then another letter.

Dear friends of my mother, whoever you are,

It's wonderful (I suppose) that you're going to take me in. There's nothing I want more than to start living with strangers, but that sounds nasty, and actually I really appreciate your offer, at least I know my mother does, and as soon as I get myself in gear, I'll appreciate it too, and be with you in no time flat. I can't tell you right now when that will be, but be assured one of these days I'll make a move. I haven't figured out yet why I'm so slow, you might even call it reluctant; I really wonder about myself, maybe I'm a total basket case, one of those people who can't stand getting what they want. Do you think that could be it? Eight years times fifty-two weeks times seven days equals 2,912 days. It's possible that I wished for my parents' return on at least 2,812 of those days. So whatsamatter with me? If you can tell me, rush your reply. Sincerely yours, Pete Greenwood, aka Pax Connors.

And finally, the last letter.

Dear Uncle Gene,
Thanks for all the help. We've had our ups and downs, I've been a nuisance, I know, and lots of times not very nice—you might even say I've been pretty rotten to you on occasion, and you've always been a gentleman about everything. So, even though you probably think I'm nothing but an ungrateful wretch, it's been great knowing you and I'm glad for your sake that pretty soon you're going to see the last of the great American nuisance. Ta ta, see you soon, maybe.

"Well, let me know when you make your plans," Gene said.

I cleared my throat. "Oh, right. Absolutely. Count on it."

Thirty-four

Gene was in costume, long black dress and bonnet, when I entered the dressing room. "Hey, here's my nephew," he said to the other actors in the room.

"Looks a lot like you," someone said. Someone else smiled at me.

I bent over Gene. "Can I talk to you? Alone."

We went out into the corridor. Gene wiped his face. "I don't have much time before the next scene."

"I just want to tell you—" I cleared my throat. "I've made up my mind. I'm going there . . . I'm going to Laura."

Gene didn't say anything for a moment. Then he moved as if to go back into the dressing room. "Why are you telling me now? I've got to concentrate on the play. You're not going this minute."

"I just wanted to tell you, I made up my mind. We saw this movie in school and—" I moved my shoulders. It sounded so ridiculous. "A movie about some old people and . . . I made up my mind. So . . . I'm not going to wait for school to end."

"You saw a movie about some old people and that made up your mind?"

"I don't know if I can explain it—"

"Try."

"They were old—"

"You said that."

"I mean, all alone. Like, ah, their kids didn't care about them or anything. Listen, Laura's going through some heavy stuff. What am I supposed to do, sit around on my duff and say, 'Do it all alone, Laura. Nice knowing you; now that you're between a rock and a hard place, don't count on me for anything.' Is that what I'm supposed to do?"

"Did I say that? Would I say that? Is that what you think?"

"I don't know what to think. You haven't helped me figure this one out, that's all I know."

"Figure it out yourself. You think I've forgotten what you said? Your life is none of my business. Right? Isn't that what you said?"

We were both yelling. "She needs me! All right? All right? Anyway, I just came to tell you, to let you know. You should be relieved I'm going. You don't have to think about me anymore. You're relieved, aren't you? Come on, Gene. Truth or consequences."

"Relieved?" He smiled unpleasantly. "I put eight years into you and then you just go away like this? Just like this?" He snatched off the bonnet, then the wig. His bare head stuck out ludicrously from the neck of the black gown. "You goddamn ungrateful kid!" He slapped me in the face.

I threw up my arms.

"Laura left you on my doorstep . . . she dumped you, a little kid, and I brought you up. I did it, didn't I? Now she wants you back? The hell with her. The hell with her!" He grabbed me and I thought he was going to hit me again, but he pulled me against him and hugged me. "You can't just go away like this," he said. "I love you. I love you, goddamn it, I love you."

He was crying and then I was crying too.

Thirty-five

Dear Laura,

I was so glad to hear from you. Of course I'm going to come, I just have a few loose ends to tie up. Yes, I understand about you and Hal and I—

Dear Laura,

Hello, how are you, this is your son writing you. Yes, I'm coming to see you and stay near you, and help you through this stuff, and get to know you again, all the things you talked about in your—

Dear Laura,

You crook your finger and you expect me to come running—did it ever occur to you that I have a life, too, that I'm not eight years old anymore? Did it ever occur to you that I might be just a little pissed at the way you left me, at the way you and Hal screwed up our family and our life? Did anything ever occur to you except what you want and what you think and the traumas you're—

Dear Laura,

I've been trying to write you and getting myself hot and frustrated, ready to smash a window. You don't know that about me, do you? I have a vicious temper, but I've never been mad at you, no, not you, not you and Hal, but Gene, yes. Uncle Gene, he's been my whipping boy, I've taken my temper out on him for years, and he took it, he took it, Laura, he took it and he went right on being there for me, right on—

Dear Laura,

It's pretty weird to be writing you in jail. I can't quite get used to the idea of my mother being in jail, but I guess it's no more weird than the idea of my mother being underground. I mean, I used to just think about it like you were some kind of terrific superheroine, but lately I've been realizing that's a pretty juvenile attitude. I've been realizing quite a lot of stuff since I got your letters. I'm not sure what it all means yet. I'm not sure what it's going to be like seeing you. Listen, to be truthful—

Dear Laura,

I'm making arrangements so I can come to NYC within the next week or so. I've got to get things set about my exams, stuff like that. I've written to your friends and I guess I'll be staying there with them, at least over the summer. Hey, maybe I'll really love NYC, the Big Apple they call it, maybe I'll want to take a big bite out of the—

Thirty-six

I had told Gene I wanted to leave right away, but I delayed. I kept busy enough to tell myself I was too busy to leave just yet. Cary and I went to see the play. I wrote my mother (finally). I went around to all my teachers and made arrangements to take my exams by mail. Totie Golden insisted on taking me out to lunch one day. What did I tell her? The same thing I told them all, even Drew. As little as possible. Mostly the old habit of secrecy, but also the whole complicated thing of saying, Look, you thought my parents were dead, but it was all a crock. Actually . . .

But what I spent the most time on was wondering what I ought to do. Stay with Gene? Go to my mother? As if the question still existed.

My mother writes.

A hasty note just to say that Matt and Emily are waiting impatiently to meet you. But that's nothing compared to how I feel! I'm getting to know some of the women here and they are all happy for me that you're coming. I'm trying not to worry about the future right now. We'll talk about it all, but at the moment what I want is to know you're near me again.

I put the letter on my bureau. Every morning I read it. And, then, as I lace up my sneakers, as I go down the stairs, as I pour a glass of milk and smear jelly on bread, as if it were a story I'm telling myself, I imagine possible endings to this part of my life.

I wait up for Gene to come home from the theater. "Gene," I say, as soon as he walks in, "I'm staying. This is my real life. Maybe I didn't know it before, but now I do. You've been father, mother, and uncle to me. I go to school here. I have Cary here, and Martha, my room, you, especially you—I know I've never said it before, I didn't say it that day at the theater, but Gene, I love you too."

We're all at the airport, waiting for my flight to be called. At my feet is a small suitcase. My mother needs me. She needs my support, my encouragement, my love. The flight is announced. Gene and I shake hands and I say, "I'll come back. I promise you that." "I know," Gene says. "You'll visit me. Once a year, you'll visit me." I want to say, "Please understand! Don't you see how it is?" I don't say it. We shake hands again. Martha kisses me. Cary and I hug. I go on the plane. I look back and see them all at the window, waving.

Fantasy immobilizes me. I must go. I have to stay. My mother is waiting. I'm going to hurt Gene too much . . . what a seesaw! I'm seasick, my thoughts pitch and rock and I can't make a move.

One day I dig the scraps from the manila envelope out of my wastebasket and spend hours piecing and Scotch-taping them together. Some I get back almost whole, some remain fragments.

* * *

"Pete," Gene says at breakfast one morning, "would it make it easier if I drove you?"

"Drove me?"

"Sure, we'll have a nice trip in the Volvo."

"I can take the bus."

"It's a ten hour trip. Forget it. We can afford a plane ticket. Anyway, that's not what I meant." He hesitates. "Last week, when you came to see me in the theater? I was unfair to you. I put the pressure on. Consider it off. I want you to do what's right for you."

"I don't know what's right for me!" I say miserably.

"You've missed Laura."

"Yes. And . . . no. I mean I have, but I keep wondering who it is I missed. I don't know her, Gene. Part of me doesn't even believe she's back. Anyway, she's someone different, and so am I. Yeah, I want to see her, but—" I push aside my plate. "Damn it! Damn it, Gene. Do you think it's easy just *going?*"

"No, I don't think that. You have friends here, Cary—"

"And you? I guess you think that part is easy for me."

"I'm not sure. I don't know what to think."

"Well, we never—we don't say things to each other, but—" My throat thickens. "You know what you said to me?" I put out my hand. "I say it back to you. Gene, I love you."

The night after the play closes, Gene takes Martha and me out to dinner. "A farewell dinner for you, Pete."

"My name is Pax." I didn't know I was going to say it. I don't know if I mean it. Why is my name Pax any more than Pete? I have to think about this. Pax Martin Gandhi Connors—that's a whole lot of name.

That's a whole lot of responsibility. I kind of like it, when I step aside and think about it. But I want to be sure that I don't carry those names around lightly. I pretty much believe in what Gandhi and Martin Luther King believed in—nonviolence, not hurting other people. I believe it, but I don't know if I'm up to living that way. Maybe I'm just an ordinary Pete after all.

Gene drinks a lot of wine at the dinner. "I don't know what I'm going to do without him," he says, putting his arm around me. He doesn't use my name all evening. "Martha!" he cries. "I want a kid, I want a child."

"Is that a proposal, sir?"

"Okay," Gene says, "okay, let's talk about it." No one laughs.

"Cary, hi, I'm going tomorrow."

"We have to write each other."

"I will if you will."

"I will, Pete. And I'm going to come visit you, don't forget that."

"I thought I was supposed to visit you."

"I'm not going to wait for you, friend. What if you forget?"

"I definitely won't."

"Good-bye, Pete."

"Cary—"

"No, I'm going to hang up right now. You too."

In the car with Gene, we drive east into the sunrise. With each hour, I'm miles closer to my mother. Why do I feel numb? Feel nothing? Sleep so much and, even when awake, feel that I'm dreaming? For all these years, above all else, I waited for this moment to arrive. This happy moment. This happy ending.

We stay overnight in a motel stuck between two highways. All night the trucks roar past and the man in the room next door coughs. "No, I slept all right," Gene says as we eat breakfast in a diner, but there are heavy lines under his eyes. We drive again. I say I wish I had my license. Gene agrees with me. We talk about school, college, Cary, Martha. Everything, in fact, but my mother.

"New York City ahead," Gene says, throwing money into the toll basket.

I look out the window. Soon I'll see her. It's true. I'll see my mother. A great wave of happiness blows over me. "Gene!" I turn to him to tell him, to share the moment. He looks at me and smiles. And then I want to cry, I want to say, Don't take me there, Gene. Take me home!

Home? Where's that? Home to my mother? Home to Gene? At that moment, I finally understand that there is no ending for my story . . . no perfect ending . . . no little-Pax-happy-at-last ending.

NORMA FOX MAZER grew up in Glens Falls, New York. She has been writing all her life and is the author of many highly acclaimed books for young readers, including TAKING TERRI MUELLER, winner of the 1981 Edgar Award for Best Young Adult Mystery, and MRS. FISH, APE, AND ME, THE DUMP QUEEN, both available from Avon Books. Her other award winning books include SATURDAY, THE TWELFTH OF OCTOBER, winner of the Lewis Carroll Shelf Award, DEAR BILL, RE-MEMBER ME?, a New York Times Outstanding Book of the Year, an ALA Notable Book, and an ALA Best Book for Young Adults, as well as UP IN SETH'S ROOM and THE SOLID GOLD KID (coauthored with her husband, Harry Mazer) both of which were ALA Best Books for Young Adults. Ms. Mazer and her husband currently make their home in the Pompey Hills of central New York State.